THEIR AMISH STEPFATHER: AMISH ROMANCE

BOOK 8 THE AMISH BONNET SISTERS

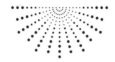

SAMANTHA PRICE

D1311040

CHAPTER ONE

From the warmth of the cozy cottage Florence shared with her husband Carter, she stood staring out the window as the chilly day faded into night. Ever since Christmas, just over a week ago, she'd spent many hours standing in that spot thinking, planning, and looking. She regretted not asking her father more questions about how he started his orchard, but it never occurred to her that she would ever need to know. Never in a million years would she have guessed she would've left the family orchard and now be an outsider looking in. So near, but yet so far.

For the past weeks, pangs of bitterness had struck her heart. As much as she'd tried to ignore them, she couldn't. It was devastating to watch her father's beloved orchard being so badly mismanaged. She'd spent as many hours praying, begging God to remove the bitterness that had settled into her heart as easily as dirt settled onto the sole of a shoe. The locals all knew the orchard as the Baker Apple Orchard because of her father.

GOD, let me get it back, she thought, mentally uttering the prayer she prayed many times a day. *Show me a way.*

It should've been hers. She had single-handedly managed it in the years after *Dat* died, and she would've felt perfectly fine if they'd allowed her to manage it for them, but to turn their backs and not even listen to her advice, was devastatingly hurtful.

In her heart, she knew she'd get her father's orchard back. She just had to. Then she'd combine the two orchards along with the one they'd bought from Mr. and Mrs. Jenkins and they'd have one huge orchard. They'd open the orchard to the local school-children again, like they used to, and teach them all about the apples—everything from growing them, classifying them, and cooking the apples.

"How about a game of chess?"

She spun around to see Carter walking out from

the kitchen. They'd already finished their early dinner. "You'll only win again."

"Yes, I will, but the fun's in the playing."

"Fun for you, but it's no fun for me knowing I'm going to lose. I'll never remember all those moves you taught me." The best she could do was remember how each piece was allowed to move, but as for strategies it was beyond her.

He chuckled and sat on the couch next to Spot. "You're worried about the orchard, aren't you?"

"I can't help it." She sank into the couch opposite.

"What would make Wilma and Levi sell to you?"

"Nothing. They don't need the money and I'm their least favorite person."

"It might be a waiting game. Waiting until they run it into the ground so to speak."

Florence tucked her legs up beside her. "I don't want it to come to that."

"From what you've said it's inevitable."

Slowly, Florence nodded. "Okay, set up the chess board and I'll try my best." Florence wasn't too keen on chess, but it made Carter so happy when he taught her.

While watching him place the pieces on the black and white squares, her thoughts drifted to her half-sisters. What would it be like living in her old family home now Wilma was married to Levi? Then there was Bliss who was also a new addition as the girls' new stepsister. How were Joy and Isaac faring as newlyweds in the household with a newly blended family? Even though the home was extra-large with many bedrooms, all those large personalities would make it seem so small.

Carter held his fists out toward her, each containing a black or a white chess piece. "Which one?"

"That one." She chose one, not bothered by the outcome.

He turned his hand over and opened it to show the piece on his palm. "White. You go first."

"You'd better watch out, one day I'll beat you."

"You could. If you put many hours into learning the game, but working to win a pointless game, as you see it, would be madness."

She laughed at him. "True. I'd rather crochet or knit. That way I have something to show for the time and effort spent."

"Well, it's not wasted hours for everyone. It paid off for me."

"It certainly did. Your chess app has given you a living, and all the people you employ."

He carried the board closer and sat on the same couch with the board between them. "Your move, Mrs. Braithwaite."

She placed one finger on the king's pawn and slid it forward two spaces.

NEWLY MARRIED, Isaac and Joy headed up the stairs of Wilma's home for an early night.

"The Bible reading starts in fifteen minutes," Levi called after them.

Joy stopped, and then walked back down two stairs so she could see her new stepfather. "We had one last night."

"My family has always had one every night."

Joy bit her tongue. "So, is this going to become a nightly thing? Isaac and I like to do our own reading in our room."

"That's right. That it will be nightly, I mean. I don't know why you all haven't done this in the past, but we're doing it starting now."

"That's because we were left to read the Bible ourselves and not be forced to do so," Cherish said.

A hush fell over the room and Joy was certain her youngest sister would get into trouble.

"It's not something you should feel forced to do. You should read the Bible because you want to."

In typical Cherish fashion she kept pushing the point. "Joy reads it more than anyone. Can't we just do it when we feel like it?"

Levi's face hardened and he looked at Wilma, who looked away. Then he rubbed his graying beard. "This is what I have set down. Every *haus* needs rules, Cherish. It seems there haven't been enough rules here before today."

"It'll be fun, Cherish. Sit next to me," said Bliss, their new stepsister.

Joy knew her stepfather disliked her. Now she was stuck there until she and Isaac had enough money for a place of their own. Having Levi taking charge made living at home nearly impossible. Since Isaac wasn't saying a thing, she had no choice but to sit down with the rest of them. Isaac stayed silent and sat next to her.

"Gather the others, Cherish," Levi ordered.

She obeyed and a minute later everyone was seated for the nightly reading. Among them was Matthew, who was staying with the family through to the end of January. Matthew was the younger brother of the two men who had married two of the older Baker sisters.

The girls had done Bible reading when their father had been alive, but it was something that just happened when someone asked a question, or something came up in conversation. They'd all gather around the fire while their father told them bedtime stories based on people in the Bible.

Joy was willing to give Levi a chance. She wanted to like him, but without talking about anything or asking anyone if they had something on their mind, he just opened the Bible and started reading at the beginning of the book of Psalms. He made no effort to make it interesting and he read in a monotone drawl. He got to the end of Psalm Five before he stopped.

"It was very interesting," Wilma said once he'd closed the book.

"Jah, Mr. Brunner, it was very good," Matthew said.

Levi smiled, gave Matthew a nod and then looked at the others in turn.

"I've always liked the Psalms." Isaac smiled.

"Why have you always liked them, Isaac?" Levi asked as though Isaac was telling a fib.

"They're full of wisdom and good messages."

"But what does it teach us?"

"To trust *Gott* to protect us," Cherish said, helping Isaac out.

"That's right."

Everyone then sat in silence for several seconds, with all eyes on Levi.

Was it okay to get up and leave now?

Joy looked up at the clock on the mantle as though willing the time to pass.

Cherish was the one who said what she figured everyone else was probably thinking, "Is that it? Can we go now?"

"You would be the one to say such a thing, Cherish." Levi then glared at Wilma. "You raised them. 'Withhold not correction from the child: for if thou beatest him with the rod, he shall not die.'"

Mamm stared at him open-mouthed.

"Cherish always was willful," Joy said. "It's not *Mamm's* fault."

"Go if you wish, Joy. I saw you weren't even listening to The Word."

Joy made to leave, and then Levi held up his hand, so she sat down again. "Have you younger girls been baptized?" he asked.

Cherish looked around nervously. She, Hope, and Favor hadn't been. "We're waiting until just before we marry, like Joy did."

"And, like Florence did?" he asked, his eyes bulging.

"Nee. Florence never got baptized."

"I know that. Your *mudder* told me." He shook his head. "You see what happened? She never made her commitment."

"No, she didn't." *Mamm* pressed her lips together. "It's true."

"It has to be our own decision, doesn't it?" Favor asked.

"Well, what is your personal decision, Favor?" Levi asked. "Do you want to leave the community like your older *schweschder?"*

Mamm leaned forward. "Excuse me. Half-*schweschder."*

Favor didn't acknowledge her mother's comment. "I don't know. I haven't even been on *rumspringa.* I'll decide what I want to do after I come back."

Joy stared at Favor. She never expected her to speak out like that and they'd never talked about *rumspringa.*

All eyes were on Levi to see what he'd say. Finally, he said, "When will you go on your *rumspringa,* Favor?"

"I don't know. I haven't really thought about it. When I'm old enough, I guess."

"Where will you live?"

"I haven't planned anything, but maybe Bliss and I could go together."

Bliss giggled but stopped when her father glared at her. She gulped and then placed her hands together on her lap. "That will be next year or the year after."

"That sounds good, doesn't it, Levi?" *Mamm* said, as though she was trying to smooth things over.

"It's the new year now. When are you planning this, Bliss?"

"*Jah,* Bliss," said Wilma, "you must have a plan and somewhere to stay and a job to support yourself."

Joy frowned at her mother. "Why all this pressure? I'm sure they'll figure it all out when the time comes."

"You shouldn't talk like that to your *mudder.*" Levi frowned at Joy.

Isaac had been quiet up until now. "Levi, Joy wasn't meaning any disrespect. But it's always been the case that no one is put under pressure for the baptism. It's their own choice."

Mamm butted in, "What you're saying is right, Isaac, but I was telling Levi only last night that I thought if Florence had only got baptized earlier, she might not have been tempted to leave us. It was too easy for her."

Joy was quiet and didn't say any more. There was really no point, but she was pleased that Isaac had finally said something.

Favor said, "She fell in love. Do you really think Florence wouldn't have married Carter if she'd been baptized?"

"We'll never know," *Mamm* said quietly.

There was another uncomfortable silence in the room. Joy looked across at Bliss to see if she'd had to put up with these conversations regularly. Bliss looked down at the floor.

"Excuse me," Cherish said. "Can we go now? I still have cleaning up to do in the kitchen."

"Jah, that's fine."

When Cherish was halfway to the kitchen, she heard Levi say, "Are you going to stay seated, Wilma, when there's work to be done? 'The hand of the diligent shall bear rule: but the slothful shall be under tribute.'"

Cherish was shocked; she turned around to see what her mother would say.

"I am feeling a little weary. One of the girls can do it."

He added, "So are we all at the end of a long day,

but there is still work that needs to be done. You must show the girls a good example, so they don't grow up lazy."

"It's all right, *Mamm*. We can all help out in the kitchen while you sit here." Favor bounded to her feet.

"Help them, Wilma, and then when all the work is done, we can all sit down here again."

Wilma pushed herself to her feet and walked to the kitchen with the girls. She knew from the girls' faces that they all felt the same about what Levi had said. He'd belittled their *Mamm* in front of them all.

Then Levi called out, "Wilma, make me and Isaac and Matthew some coffee. And make it extra hot. You never make it hot enough."

Nearly at the kitchen, Joy looked back to Isaac sitting next to Matthew. They were both looking very uncomfortable. She knew at that moment she and Isaac couldn't stay there. They had to move out, but to where?

Once Joy walked into the kitchen, she whispered, "You sit down, *Mamm*. We'll make the coffee."

"I'll do it and I'll make sure it's burning HOT!" Cherish whispered loud enough for those in the kitchen to hear. Even Bliss heard and didn't say anything. "So hot it burns his mouth off."

"Don't say that, Cherish," *Mamm* said. "It's not an easy adjustment for him to make. It's only been him and Bliss for so long."

"It's okay, Wilma," Bliss said. "He didn't mean to upset you. That's just how he is."

"So, it's not that he's making an adjustment?" Favor asked.

"Nee." She shook her head.

Cherish filled up the teakettle with water.

Joy sat down next to *Mamm* and put her arm around her shoulder. She could see *Mamm* regretted her decision to marry Levi. How could she have known he'd be this intolerable?

CHAPTER TWO

*T*he next morning, Cherish was determined to stay cheerful. She would not let Levi bring everyone down—at least, not her.

Soon everyone was in the kitchen, except for Isaac who'd left for work. As usual, the air buzzed with two different conversations.

Cherish was in charge of the cooking and she made sure that Levi's bacon was crispy and his eggs hard, just like he preferred them. Her reasoning was that if he started the day in a good mood it would be better for everyone.

When breakfast was over, and Hope was clearing the dishes from the table, Levi said, "Sit down, Hope. Before everyone leaves the breakfast table we need a family meeting."

Another one? Cherish started to groan, but she managed to stop herself before it escaped.

"Shall I stay?" asked Matthew, half standing.

"Jah, you can stay."

"I don't mind going."

"Sit, Matthew," Levi ordered.

Matthew sat.

Cherish asked as sweetly as she could, "Didn't we just have a family meeting last night?"

"Nee. That was a Bible reading to feed our souls and build up our faith. It's more important than eating. If we're not feeding the spirit what does it matter about the body?"

"But we talked," Cherish said quietly, and then immediately regretted it when Levi stared coldly at her.

"I've never come across a young lady who complains as much as you do." Then he looked at Wilma. "It seems you've spoiled her."

That really irritated Cherish. Why did everyone say she was spoiled when she clearly wasn't? She wouldn't let him see she was bothered. "I'm not complaining I'm just asking questions. I really didn't think we'd need a fixed family event every day. Last night, a Bible reading and now a family meeting." Cherish was secretly hoping to be sent to her room.

That would be better than listening to Levi droning on.

"I have something important to announce. The harvest wasn't good, and as I've taken over the family finances, I've made changes. I think you'll all agree the changes are for the betterment of all of us."

"Changes about how the orchard's being run or who's managing it?" Favor asked.

"I'll be overseeing the orchard; we all know that. There are things I have learned from the mistakes we made. We'll have to do the harvest earlier next year."

Joy said, "Florence always says you have to read the signs. You can't go by when it was done the previous year. It depends what the weather's been like during the year."

He stared at Joy. "We must choose a date. How else would we know when to get the workers here?"

"They only need to be given a day's notice. That's how we've always done things."

"You and I can argue about that later, Joy." He moved in his chair. "Things are going to be different around here. You girls have done what you've wanted for too long."

Cherish noticed Bliss was looking down at her nails, peeling one off.

"I don't know how we could save any more money than we already do," *Mamm* said.

"We have to stop spending and start bringing more money in. The money will go into the family bank account and each girl will get an allowance according to the jobs they do around here."

Hope's jaw dropped. "You mean we have to get a full-time job and do chores as well?"

"Everyone will have to work outside the home except for Wilma and Joy. Things need to be done around the *haus,* and if you girls don't do them, who will? Wilma will do the bulk of it and then she'll give you girls other chores to do while you're here. There are many things that need to be done."

"Why don't we go back to having a market stall? Or even a roadside stall. That worked well for us for years," Joy suggested.

He shook his head. "We need surer money than that. There are many jobs you girls could do. You could work in shops, work in bakeries, or as cleaners. Work in an office for those of you good with filing or number skills."

"*Nee, Dat,* in offices these days you need to have computer skills. None of us has that," Bliss said.

"I'm already working at the café," said Cherish.

"But I only get a few shifts. I've already got my name down for more, but they can't give me more hours over the winter months. They're not busy enough."

Levi grunted, "I've already told you about that, Cherish. Get another part-time job and that will equal a full-time one."

"But then I won't be available to work when they want me."

"Cherish, I know you want to argue, but I'm not your *mudder*. The Lord will bless your undertakings if your heart and your hands are willing."

Cherish blew out a deep breath when she couldn't think of a reply.

"What about all the work there is to be done around here?" Favor asked.

"We've already covered that," Bliss told her.

Favor said, "I'm not talking about the chores, I'm talking about the orchard."

"There's no work to be done in the orchard in the wintertime, only at harvest. And if you girls have got full-time jobs, other workers can help with the harvest and people in the community can come and help."

"They have to know what they're doing, though." Joy said, while Cherish nodded, agreeing.

"It's not your concern. Today, you'll all look for jobs."

"How much will the allowance be?" asked Hope.

"I will decide later."

Cherish didn't mind paying board, but she didn't want someone else getting all her money. She couldn't wait to escape to the farm. Even being around her caretaker wasn't as bad as Levi.

Levi drained the contents of his coffee mug. "Regrettably, we'll need to sell a horse or two. I brought two buggies with me and now we have four buggies and eight horses." He shook his head. "This is too many for one family."

"How would the girls get to and from their jobs?" *Mamm* asked.

By her mother's question, Cherish knew he hadn't talked anything over with her. He was making decisions by himself. Their father had always been thoughtful and considerate, and he and their mother had worked as a team. That was something Cherish hadn't realized until now.

"We'll see when the time comes. I think we only need sell one horse for now and he'll bring in a good sum of money."

"And which one will that be?" asked Hope.

"Wilbur."

"Nee!" Wilma gasped.

Everyone stared at Levi in disbelief. Wilbur had been Levi's gift to Wilma before they were courting.

CHAPTER THREE

*C*herish looked at her mother, as did the other girls. Wilbur was a fine horse, their best. He'd been Florence's favorite too. And he belonged to *Mamm.* It made Cherish resent Levi all the more. "How much would he be?" Cherish wondered if she might find a way to buy him and have him taken to her farm.

"We'll have to see what kind of offers we get. I'll put the word out that he's for sale."

"Why not put him for sale through the auction, *Dat?*" Bliss asked.

Cherish narrowed her eyes at her. Didn't she know how they'd come by the horse? Bliss didn't even notice her new stepsister scowling at her.

"We'd have to pay the auction fee. We won't have

to pay any fees if we find someone among our friends to take him off our hands," Levi answered.

"We get to keep all the other horses and all the other buggies?" Hope asked.

"That's right. For now, anyway."

"When do we have to get jobs by?" Hope asked.

"You can all go out today and find yourselves jobs."

"It might not be that easy," Favor said.

He stared at Favor. "Whoever *does not* want to *work* should not be allowed to *eat*." Then he looked around at all of them. "Is there anyone here who does not want to work?" Everyone was silent. "If you don't work you won't get anything from this *haus*."

"*Jah*," said Wilma. "The Lord blesses those who put effort into things."

Hope stood. "I guess we should make an early start."

"What about Bliss?" asked Cherish.

"She's included," her father said.

"I'm not well today." Bliss put her hand to her forehead.

Wilma butted in, "Since you're only mentioning it now you're not staying home."

Bliss breathed out heavily, then stared at her

father, but he wasn't giving her any sympathy or a way out.

Bliss, Hope, Favor and Cherish got ready for their day of job-searching.

WITH ISAAC HAVING ALREADY GONE to work, Joy stayed in the kitchen with her mother while the girls hitched the buggy. *"Mamm,* Wilbur's your horse," she whispered so Levi wouldn't hear.

"I know, but he's right about us having too many."

"He gave Wilbur to you as a gift and now he's taking him away. How's that right?"

Mamm fixed a smile on her face. "He's going to be the saving of this family."

"Levi is?" Joy made a face. She'd been thinking the opposite. He'd already ruined one harvest. "Is he going out today?"

"He's going to visit some people to see if they want to buy Wilbur."

"Are you going with him?"

"Ach nee! He wouldn't like that. I'll have to stay home and work."

Joy knew she was getting it much easier than the other girls because she was married. Levi saw Joy as

Isaac's problem. "When he goes out, you have a lie down. You look so tired."

"That would be deceitful."

"Only if he asks. I mean, he won't ask if you've been cleaning the *haus* all the time since he's been gone. I'll do the cleaning for us both."

Mamm drew her lips together. "I am a little tired."

Joy sighed. "I hope the girls can find jobs."

"I thought all my worries would be over when I got married. We must pray for a miracle, Joy."

Joy nodded but couldn't see how that miracle could come. Unless *Gott* could work on Levi's heart, but a complete change of personality was what was needed, and that was a big project.

When the girls drove away from the house heading into town, Cherish tried to figure out how she was going to get out of it. Finding jobs would be boring and it could take all day. Besides, she was happy with her three shifts at the café. That was all she needed for pocket money. "Ooh, my tummy."

"What's the matter?" Bliss asked Cherish.

"I've not been feeling well all day. It's my women's problem."

"That's too bad. Do you want a blanket?" Bliss picked up a colorful one that Mercy and Honor had crocheted for the buggy.

"*Nee.* I need to get out into the open air."

"Do you want me to stop the buggy?" Hope glanced over her shoulder at Cherish.

"*Jah.* Let me out here and I'll walk home."

Favor, who was sitting beside her in the backseat, put her hand on her shoulder. "We can drive you back. It's no trouble."

"*Nee.* I'll feel better to walk. The motion's making me nauseous."

"Take her home, Hope," Favor said.

"The walk will do her good. It always helps me when I feel like that." Hope said as she pulled the buggy off the road.

"How do you know she's not faking it?" Bliss asked, staring straight at Cherish.

"*Nee,* she wouldn't," Favor said.

As soon as the horse came to a halt, Cherish got out and then held her stomach. "I'll see you this afternoon. I'll need to go home and rest. A slow walk and a lie down should fix me and if I feel a little better, I'll help *Mamm* and Joy with the chores. I'm sure Levi wouldn't want me to lie down in the freezing buggy all day while you girls go looking for work."

"Take the blanket," Hope said. "It's so cold out. Your coat won't be enough."

"Denke," Cherish took the colorful blanket and threw it about her shoulders.

Hope clicked her tongue and moved the reins and the horse moved onward leaving Cherish by the roadside.

Cherish had to conceal a smile that ached to break out. She needed to forget all about the ogre that now ruled her household, and have some fun. To her, that meant she needed some male attention to brighten up her day. The closest man who fit that bill was Fairfax, their *Englisher* neighbor.

CHAPTER FOUR

ather than walk along the road and risk running into Levi, she headed cross-country. Wrapping the blanket tight around herself, she thought about Fairfax and how he'd knocked on their door recently. At first, he'd seemed to like Joy, but back then he didn't know Joy was about to get married. Now, Joy *was* married.

Hope had a mad crush on Fairfax and talked about him often. Perhaps she could match them together. Fairfax wasn't her type at all, but she was curious about him and the lifestyle of outsiders in general.

Eventually, she reached Fairfax's family orchard and walked past the main house toward the cottage. She stepped up on the porch and knocked on the door of the quaint dark blue cottage. When there was no answer, she walked around the entire building knocking on the white back doors and peeking in through the white framed windows.

When she looked through a bedroom window, she saw one mattress on the floor, one wardrobe and one television. In the living room were two wooden crates and a dining table with no chairs. She saw what looked like coffee cups on the table.

"I guess he's not home," she muttered to herself in disappointment.

Wondering what to do next, she walked back down the driveway. She definitely didn't want to go back home and be faced with a grumpy Levi or her worried-looking mother, who had aged at least ten years in a few weeks of marriage. Wilma looked every bit the grandmother that she would become when Cherish's two sisters gave birth in a couple of months.

Cherish's breath caught in her throat when she saw a woman. It had to be Fairfax's mother.

She smiled and walked toward the woman. She was wearing some kind of a riding outfit—cream jodhpurs, a well-tailored and fitted coat, and long black boots that ended just under the knee.

The woman looked up at her. "Can I help you?"

"Oh, not really. I was just seeing if Fairfax was home."

The woman narrowed her eyes just slightly but not in a threatening way. "Are you a friend of his?"

"We do know each other, of course. Otherwise I wouldn't be here."

She laughed. "I'm his mother. I know so few of his friends these days. We used to be very close but now he's closer with his friends. I guess that's what happens. With him being an only child, I've got nothing to gauge it by." The woman smiled at Cherish and Cherish warmed to her immediately.

"Are you going riding?" Cherish asked, now feeling a little silly in the brightly colored blanket that was wrapped around her.

"I've got my last show jumping competition coming up in a few days."

"Oh, that sounds so interesting. I'd never be allowed to do that. We don't even ride horseback."

The woman pointed to a paddock full of white and red horse jumps. "That's my practice area. I've only got another year before we're moving and then I'll have to sell my horses."

"That is sad. Will you really have to sell them?"

"My husband insists that we should retire and move to Florida. I could keep them somewhere rather than sell, but I'd probably never get to see them."

"I went there once, to Florida I mean, many years ago. To a wedding. It was in Pinecraft."

"I don't know that area."

"It's very pretty. Very different from here."

"This place was my dream and my husband allowed me to have it for so long. Now it's his turn to do what he wants, and he wants Florida."

"That sounds fair."

"Do you live on the apple orchard?"

"Yes. I do. My name's Cherish, by the way. Sorry, I should have said so sooner."

"I'm pleased to meet you, Cherish. We met your father once."

She grimaced. "Levi?"

"I don't think Levi was his name."

"Oh. You must mean my real father. I have a step-father now. My mother remarried just a few weeks ago."

"Yes, I did hear your father died some years ago, and I'm sorry about that. We did send flowers."

"I didn't know. Thank you. I really didn't know what was going on back then... I was pretty young. I was told who sent what. We had a lot of flowers come from people *Dat* knew."

"I lost my father when I was a young girl, in my mid-teenage years. It was a very confusing time for me. But a couple of years later, I met a wonderful man and we got married."

"It sounds like a perfect love story."

"It has been." They exchanged smiles.

"Well, I won't hold you up. I'll be needed back home."

"Yes, I better get riding before the rain comes." She looked up at the sky. "Do you want me to tell Fairfax you were here when I see him?"

"No, it's fine."

"Goodbye, Cherish."

"Goodbye, Mrs. Jenkins. It was lovely to meet you, finally." Cherish started to walk away.

"Thank you. And I'm pleased to have met you, Cherish. Do stop by again."

Looking over her shoulder, Cherish said, "Thanks, I will." It was a pleasant surprise how nice Fairfax's mother was. She'd always thought a certain way about outsiders, but Fairfax was pleasant and so was his mother.

ot ready to go home, Cherish bypassed her house and made her way through the orchard to Florence's place.

All the way there, she thought about how awful her homelife was now. She arrived at Florence's on the verge of tears.

Florence opened the door and stared at her.

"What is it, Cherish?"

"When I got back from the farm, I found out about Levi's new rule."

"Go on."

"We all have to get jobs and work five days a week. I don't even know if the café can give me five days' work a week—all day long. That means I'll have to get a second part-time job and I might lose

35

the first one. So, do I quit my part-time job at the café, and look for a full-time job somewhere?"

"So, this applies to all of you? Even Wilma?"

Cherish shook her head, and then Florence led her in to sit in front of the fire. With a swoop of her hand, Cherish moved the blanket from around her shoulders to cover her knees. "It doesn't apply to Wilma, but he expects her to do everything around the place, and she's not used to it."

"How is she keeping up?"

"I don't think she is. She does have Joy to help her. Whenever Levi is about, he won't even let Joy cook. I made him breakfast this morning, but I'm sure he thought Wilma should've done it. He didn't say anything. He just looked at Wilma with a grumpy face."

"That's terrible. I know how Joy likes to cook for Isaac, can't she do that now?"

"No."

"How's Isaac getting along with everybody now that he's living in the house?"

"You know Isaac, he gets along with everyone."

"Yes, he does."

"Tell me what to do, Florence. What do I do about a job?"

"You just have to keep your part-time job until

you find a full-time job. And what will become of the orchard? Who's in charge of that?"

"No one."

Florence was upset. "It's not going to last with him running it."

"Oh, don't say that."

"I'm only saying it because it's true. I don't know what will become of it. But it can't last if it's not being properly worked."

Cherish said, "I know it, but I don't like to think about it. All *Dat's* hard work and all your hard work."

"It's awful. I try to put what happened at harvest time out of my mind. It's the last thing I want to think of as well."

Cherish put her hand on Florence's arm. "It must be hard for you to be so close and not be able to go near it. I wish she wasn't so stubborn."

Florence knew the 'she' Cherish was talking about was Wilma. "I put it out of my mind for the most part and think about our own orchard we'll soon have."

"You're still going ahead with that, then?"

"Yes. I'm not going to let anyone put me off it."

"Good for you." Cherish peeped out from under her lashes. "Need a worker around here?"

Florence laughed. "I don't at the moment until the planting starts and that'll be a long way off. Eric Brosley's helping us plan the drainage and he'll show us what to do. Who knows, maybe one day we'll need a worker."

"I'll be living at the farm by then. I'm seriously thinking of the emancipation thing that Malachi told me about."

"Ooh, I wouldn't mention that around *Mamm.*"

"I won't unless I'm getting pushed too far. How come Levi isn't thinking this through?"

"I guess he thinks that the orchard will just run itself. How does Wilma feel about doing all the bulk of the work around the *haus?*"

"*Mamm* doesn't say anything, but she goes to bed right after she's done the dinner wash up."

"That doesn't sound good. She always used to stay up with me until late."

"*Nee.* Not anymore. I don't think she's happy."

"She wouldn't be. She wouldn't know why you girls can't help her. I wonder why Levi thinks as he does."

"Who would know? The worst of it all is Bliss doesn't have to do anything."

"What?"

"That's right. She doesn't have to do anything

because she gets these headaches, you see. Migraines... and they make her incapable of working."

"Yes, I had a couple of migraines once. I know how debilitating that can be."

Cherish frowned at Florence. "They're not real. Hers aren't, I mean. She's just made them up."

"How do you know?"

Cherish got up and warmed her back by the fire. "They only started when she and Levi moved into the *haus*. I don't mind working every day. I like to be kept busy, but I just worry about the orchard. And how long will *Mamm* be able to carry on doing everything herself?"

"It must be hard on her to do all the work. And now there's extra work with Bliss and Isaac there."

"And Matthew. He's staying until the end of the month."

"He is?"

"*Jah.*"

"Is he having a vacation?"

Cherish shrugged her shoulders. "I secretly think they're trying to match Hope with him."

"Isn't he younger?"

"Don't know. Never cared enough to ask, but he creates more work. It's so unfair. I'm just looking forward to leaving someday." She stared at Florence. "What would I do without the farm? I'm so grateful Dagmar left it to me."

"You are blessed."

"I know. And if she had left it to all us girls like *Mamm* said she should've, then Levi might've stepped in and ruined it."

Florence nodded. "I don't doubt it. Do you want a cup of coffee?"

"I'd love one. Do you want me to make it for us?"

Florence had a flashback of the last time Cherish had been in her kitchen. She'd left pieces of the coffee machine all over the countertop. "No, I'll get it."

They left Spot on his couch and moved to the kitchen. "It's still warm in here."

Florence giggled. "Central heating. We only have the fire on because we like an open fireplace."

"Electric heating?" Cherish looked around.

Florence shook her head. "No, it's heated with natural gas. It's much more economical than electricity for that."

Cherish sat on one of the countertop stools. "This is such a beautiful kitchen."

"It is. Thank you. Carter designed it. You've seen it before, though."

"I know, I liked it then, too. Where is Carter?"

"He's upstairs working."

"Oh, I won't disturb him. What will I do, Florence?"

"About working?"

"Yes, well, about the whole thing. Levi is creating chaos for everyone."

Florence measured out the coffee. "While you're living there, you'll have to abide by his rules. I don't see there's any way around it, unless Wilma can talk to him about it. Have you talked with her?"

"No, I haven't been getting on very well with her lately. I talked to her once about it and she actually covered her ears."

"You might have to do what he says. Just make the most of it, the best of it."

Cherish groaned. "It's not fair."

"Oftentimes life's not fair. The tough times are meant to teach us things."

"Don't start. You're sounding exactly like Joy."

"It's true."

"It might be, but it's not what I want to hear."

Florence smiled at Cherish as she flicked the switch for the coffee.

Once they were back in front of the fire with coffee and cookies, Cherish said, "Okay, I wasn't gonna tell you this, but you might as well know. He said if we don't work five days a week, he won't let us eat."

"I'm sure he didn't mean it. He's not going to let anyone starve. Just go along with it. You've really got no choice."

Cherish sighed and reached for another cookie. "I wish *Mamm* had never married him. He wasn't so bad before, but now that he's married, he's awful."

"Maybe he's trying to improve everyone's lives and teach responsibility."

"I own a farm, I already know about responsibility."

"I know, but you don't know what he's heard."

"Who from?"

"He could've heard something that *Mamm* said and he's taking it the wrong way."

"Do you think *Mamm* said something mean about us and he believes it?"

"I didn't mean it as strongly as that, but maybe the man was cross with one of you one day and she said something, and he's taken it to heart, and he thinks he's doing good. She could've said that you're lazy or something."

"I suppose that's possible. I shouldn't think so poorly of him."

"Be patient with him. It's not easy walking into a household with so many children, especially almost-grownup children, and trying to adjust. He's probably just finding his place and seeing where he fits. It must be a lot of responsibility becoming the head of a household."

"Well, you know about that because you were the head of the household for so long. Is it a lot of responsibility?"

"It is, but I've kind of grown up with it. I didn't step from one family into another family. Especially not a second-marriage family."

"I see what you mean." Cherish nibbled on her cookie. "I'll try to be patient, but I don't know if I will be successful at it."

Florence sat next to her and sipped her coffee. "No, it's not easy but it's best if you just give him some leeway for a few months and do everything he wants. Remember how hard it is for him. Who knows what expectations Wilma has put on him?"

Cherish shook her head. "I'm sure it's the other way around. He's put the expectations on her to do everything. Normally all of us girls help her, and you know how Joy has cooked the evening meals ever since Isaac started coming to dinner every night?"

"I know. I'm sure Isaac and Joy can't wait to get out of there either and get into a place of their own."

"Probably." After she had another sip of coffee, she asked, "Do you have any more cookies?"

"I sure do." Florence headed back to the kitchen and opened a new packet of chocolate chip cookies.

Once she set them down in the living room, Cherish looked up at Florence. "Don't you bake these days?"

"No, not very often. Carter has taken over the cooking. He enjoys it."

Cherish took a large bite of cookie and looked around munching before she swallowed it. "Your life has certainly changed."

Before Florence could comment, Cherish noticed the small clock on the mantelpiece. "Is that the time?" She jumped up to look closer.

"It is. Do You have to be somewhere?"

"Home. I'm meant to be sick."

"You are?"

Cherish rushed over and threw the blanket around her shoulders. "It's a long story. Thanks for the coffee and cookies. I'll give you an update on Levi next time I see you. Say hello and goodbye to Carter for me?"

"I will."

Florence hurried over to hug her and then after the quick embrace, Cherish was gone. She stood at the window and watched Cherish get smaller and smaller as she hurried away. When Florence looked at the clock, she noticed Cherish hadn't even asked who was in the photo that sat beside the clock. It was a photo of Florence's mother. It was typical of Cherish to be consumed by what was going on in her own world, and not inquire about anyone else's life.

CHAPTER SIX

*L*ater that night at the Baker home, Joy and Isaac were talking in their bedroom before they went down to join the others for dinner.

"It's not very nice here." Joy was upset with Levi's new rules that their mother had to do the bulk of the work at home.

"It's okay. We'll have our own place soon."

"And that will be when? Never, with what Levi's charging us for board. The whole idea of us living here was so that we could save money and now …"

"Don't say it." Isaac pressed a finger lightly against Joy's lips.

She grabbed his hand and held onto it. "I know you're thinking it too. It just makes me so upset.

Mamm goes along with anything, saying he is the head of the household."

"It doesn't help if we get upset about it. We must remain happy and positive and not dwell on what irritates us."

"We might as well just move out. Would we be paying any more if we did?"

He shook his head. "It would work out about the same."

"Can't you talk to him, man-to-man?"

"Already did. When he told me how much we'd be paying for the two of us to live here."

"It's outrageous. Do you think we should go to your sister's? I'm sure Christina and Mark wouldn't mind if we lived there."

"I just moved out and I don't want to move back in. It is a small *haus.*"

"I know, and this place is so large, and it's got so many rooms. I don't see any point staying here, though. Not when we have the aggravation of other people around and it's best that we start our married life together with just us two, don't you think?"

"Of course I do. I want to be alone with you. I'll look for a place if that's what you want."

"I do, *denke.* I can't wait to move out. Tomorrow is

Saturday, let's get far away from here and I'll pack us a picnic."

He shook his head. "Can't do it."

"Why not, you're not working tomorrow, are you?"

"I'm not, but I told Levi I'd help him clean out the barn."

That news did nothing to improve her mood. "Well, is he going to pay you or take some money off the rent?"

Isaac chuckled. "I don't think so."

"Isaac, it's not funny. Now he's got you working as well as paying top money for rent."

"He's your step-*vadder*, I don't want to upset him or your *mudder*."

She stared at him. One thing she loved about him was his sweet and easy-going nature, but it also had the downside that he didn't always speak up for what was right. Tomorrow, she would have a straightforward conversation with her mother.

THE NEXT DAY, Joy took her opportunity. Even though it was a Saturday all the girls left to look for work again and Levi and Isaac set to work in the barn. Joy helped her mother in the kitchen. A day of baking was what they had planned.

"*Mamm*, wasn't the idea of me staying here with Isaac so we could save money for a place of our own?"

"That's right."

"We're not saving money when your new husband is charging us a lot of rent."

"That's no concern of mine. That's between him and you. If you think it's too high, have a talk with him. Don't come to me and talk with me behind his back. This conversation is over."

"You are my *mudder*. You're the one who suggested we stay here to save money."

Wilma stopped kneading the bread dough. "Why do you girls always put pressure on me?"

"It's too much. It's just too much." All the pent-up emotion sent Joy running to her room leaving her mother to do the baking by herself. It took her a good twenty minutes to calm down before she went back. She couldn't let her mother do all that work by herself.

Nothing further was said.

CHAPTER SEVEN

On Monday, Florence and Carter were in a furniture store looking for a new office chair for Carter when Florence saw a familiar person walking past the shop window. "It's Favor."

Florence went outside to talk with her, and Carter followed. When they caught up with her, they exchanged hugs. "What are you doing in this part of town?"

"I'm looking for a job. We've all got to get jobs now."

Florence kept quiet about Cherish visiting her recently and telling her the same news. "Why's that?"

"Levi's rules. We have to work five or six days a

week now, and he doesn't like the idea of a roadside stall or the markets like we used to do."

"And how is the job hunting going?" Carter asked.

"Not good for me. And I don't know about the orchard and what's happening with it. Last harvest was a complete disaster. I don't know what's going to happen. At this rate, we will all be leaving home at the first chance we get. We don't even get to keep any of our money when we get jobs."

"None of it?" asked Carter.

"I don't think so. Probably not much. Levi said he'll work out an allowance and all the money we earn goes into the family account."

Florence didn't want to say too much so she just nodded.

"And the worst thing is he's selling Wilbur!"

Florence couldn't believe her ears. "What? Why?"

"For no good reason. Because he needs to get some money for the family, that's what he said."

"What does Wilma think about that?"

"The same thing she thinks about everything—nothing. You might not know, Carter, but Wilbur was a gift to her from Levi."

"I can't see that she'd be very happy about selling him."

Favor chewed on the end of a fingernail. "I hope he goes to a good home. You could buy him, couldn't you?"

"We'd love to, but I don't think it will be practical. Carter just gave away his cows to make way for the orchard, so I don't think would be a good idea to replace the cows with a horse."

"I know but it's Wilbur."

"He's selling him because he needs money?" asked Carter.

"He said we've got too many buggy horses now that the two families are combined. I don't know why he couldn't have sold one of the other horses. Probably because he thought he could get the most money for Wilbur."

"Well, he is a fine horse and younger than the others. He probably could get the most money for him. Does he have a buyer yet?"

"I don't know. He only told us over breakfast that he was going to sell him."

"We better let you get on with your job searching."

"Alright."

. . .

THAT AFTERNOON while Carter stayed upstairs making plans for the weekend get-together he was arranging for Florence to meet his staff, Florence sat in front of the fire beginning her new knitting project of making a scarf for Carter. As she cast on the stitches, she couldn't stop thinking about Wilbur. She didn't know if Wilbur was her stepmother's most favored horse or whether Wilma even had a favorite, but he sure was her favorite.

"BONNET SISTER WARNING." Carter called out from upstairs.

"Don't call them that." Florence laughed. When she opened the door, she wasn't at all surprised to see Cherish standing there.

"Cherish, what has Malachi done this time?" Florence expected Cherish to complain about the young man who was looking after her farm. She held the door opened to allow her inside.

Cherish marched past, took off her coat and then handed it to Florence. While Florence hung it up, Cherish said, "He's probably done something, but I don't know what it is. I'm here to tell you about someone else."

Florence knew she meant Levi. "Let's sit. Coffee?"

"Nee. You'll never guess what Levi's done now."

"I think I might. He's selling *Mamm's* horse."

"That's right. How did you know?"

"I ran into Favor in town a couple hours ago and she told me."

"And you do remember it was a special gift to her, right?"

"I remember. I was right there on the very day listening to the conversation when he gave him to her."

"And he never said he was going to take him back." Cherish shook her head.

"No, he didn't."

"I'm quite upset about that and *Mamm* didn't even have a say. Is that how marriage is supposed to work?" Without waiting for a response, she grabbed Florence's arm. "What are we going to do? Can you buy him?"

"I was thinking of it, but the thing is, I can't have a horse here. I've got no stables, no pasture anymore, and when the winter passes, we'll be digging, doing drainage for our trees."

They both heard someone clearing their throat

and turned around to see Carter at the bottom of the stairs.

"I'm sorry, I overheard. The walls and the floor are thin, apparently. We could have a horse if you want, Florence."

"It'd be too much trouble."

"We don't have to keep him here. We could keep the horse at the Jenkinses' place. They've got plenty of pasture, stables, and a big barn. I'm sure they wouldn't mind."

"Yes, they do, and Mrs. Jenkins already has horses. She might not mind one extra."

"I never thought of that."

Cherish clapped her hands together. "That sounds great."

"But wait a minute. Levi would never agree to selling a horse to me. I don't think he's happy with me at the moment." She didn't say it out loud, that she always felt Levi didn't like her even when she was still in the community.

"What if one of the Jenkinses was the buyer? Someone such as their son?"

Was Cherish up to her old tricks? Florence narrowed her eyes. "What do you know about the Jenkins boy?"

"I met him the other day when he came looking

for you. And then I was at his place, the cottage. He doesn't have any furniture in it yet, but it looks good."

"Are you saying to ask Fairfax to buy the horse on our behalf and keep hidden from Levi the fact that he's doing the buying for us?" Carter asked.

"Yes. Give him the money, he can buy the horse and then keep him at the Jenkinses' place. Levi will never have to know. When the Jenkinses move to Florida, the horse stays."

"Do you think he'll do it?" Carter asked.

"I could ask him." Cherish smiled brightly.

"It's deceptive." Florence tried to weigh up the moral rights and wrongs of the situation.

"It is… a bit. But he shouldn't be selling the horse anyway. I would like to buy him, if I had the money, and give him back to Wilma, but I know that wouldn't go over very well. I couldn't bear it if he went some place where he was mistreated or handled roughly."

"I think Levi just wants him to go for a lot of money. He didn't mention he was concerned for his welfare. He'd think he was just a horse."

"We can buy him if you want," Carter said to Florence.

"Does it make sense for us to have a horse?"

He smiled. "It does if you want one. We don't have to keep him here. Perhaps you should make the arrangements with him, Cherish."

Florence stared at Carter. "Really? Make arrangements with who?"

"Fairfax. Like Cherish said." He turned his gaze to Cherish. "See if he'll go along with your scheme," he said to her.

Florence was doubtful. "I'm not sure it's a good idea."

"Buying and selling things is something she'll need to do when she has her farm. Besides, I have a feeling Cherish would be good at making these arrangements."

"Thanks, Carter. I'm certain he'll do it. And I'll make sure he gets the horse at a very good price for you."

"I'll pay a fair price for him," said Carter. "I just want to make sure we get him."

Cherish shook her head. "We will not pay one dollar more than we have to."

Carter chuckled and looked over at Florence. "See what I mean?"

Florence nodded. She knew money wasn't a problem for Carter. He was always telling her they had plenty of money, but she never knew how much.

It was odd not to be in charge of the finances because after her father died, she had managed everything for her family. In a way, it was nice not to carry that burden.

Cherish jumped to her feet and hurried toward the door, slipped into her coat and faced them. "I'm going to see Fairfax right now."

Florence nodded and hoped this wasn't going to blow up in their faces. When Carter went back upstairs Florence turned her attention to the weekend coming. Every single person from Carter's work, and each one's spouse, was coming to the weekend he'd arranged. She'd been working at learning names, but it wasn't easy without the faces to match them to. Carter was putting them all up in a hotel for the weekend as a post-Christmas celebration. It was really intended as a time for Florence to meet everyone.

CHAPTER EIGHT

*C*herish hurried through the orchard, past Fairfax's parents' place, and made it to the door of the cottage. She was just about to knock when she heard Fairfax's voice. Looking around, she saw him in front of a row of stables, waving a shovel in the air.

"What are you doing here?" he asked.

She made her way over. "What are you doing?"

"Mucking out the stables. This is one of my jobs."

Cherish grimaced as she looked at the large mound of manure. "That's the worst job ever."

"Oh, it's not so bad. Makes great fertilizer for the vegetables."

"I hate it."

"What can I do for you, Cherish?"

"I'm glad you asked, because now I know that you would like to do something for me. Not for me alone, many people will be happy if you do this thing."

He set down the shovel and leaned against the wall of the barn. "I'm listening. Sounds like a long story."

"Not too long. Recently my mother married someone, and he has just decided to get rid of everyone's favorite horse. His name's Wilbur."

"Your mother's new husband is named Wilbur? And he's—"

"No! Wilbur's the horse, and Levi is the husband who's decided to get rid of him."

"Oh, that's too bad. And … you're telling me this, why?"

"Because—"

"You want me to do something about it?"

"Exactly. You're very good at guessing."

"I try."

"Carter and Florence, who actually own this place, want to buy the horse."

"That's great, problem solved. Isn't it?"

"Well it would be if we were dealing with normal people, but we're not; we're dealing with a very stubborn Amish man who doesn't like Florence and Carter because they're outsiders."

"Ah, I see where you're coming from. He wouldn't sell to them or would do so grudgingly or maybe at a high price but if a stranger like me comes along, there's a good chance he might sell the horse to me. I know a few people like that. Is that where I come into it?"

"Exactly."

He frowned. "Why didn't Carter ask me himself, or Florence?"

"Because I offered. They're quite busy with everything they've got going on."

"And you've got all the time in the world?"

"I have a part-time job, but soon I'll have a full-time job and be working like a slave. Anyway, what do you say?"

He gave a lopsided smile. "Where do you work?"

"At the café next to the post office. Do you know it?"

"I've never noticed it. Anyway, what do I have to do? About Wilbur, I mean."

"I think … you knock on our door, ask to speak to Levi, and then say you heard he has a good buggy horse for sale."

He chuckled. "Is he going to believe I want to buy the horse?"

"If he asks, just say you want to learn harness racing and you think he might be a good practice horse."

"It doesn't sound very believable to me."

"It doesn't have to be believable to you, it has to be believable to Levi. He's not too bright."

Fairfax laughed. "I like it how whatever you're thinking comes straight out of your mouth."

"Not all of it."

He laughed again. "That's a worry. That's even worse."

"So, will you do it?"

He straightened up and dusted off his hands. "So how much am I paying for this horse and how will I get the money to him if he agrees to sell?"

"I'm sure you can pay him cash, but he hasn't set a price for the horse yet. He said he wants to see what kind of offers he gets. Just show your interest and go from there. But I don't want Carter to have to give my stepfather a lot of money, but neither do I want him to miss out on the horse."

"This isn't going to be some long drawn out thing, is it?"

"Oh." She stepped back. "I told Carter you wouldn't mind. I'll have to look for somebody else."

"Hey, wait a minute! I'll do it. I'm just trying to assess the difficulty of the situation. I'm assuming your new stepfather is Amish?"

"Through and through. I thought I already said that."

"How's he going to like me knocking on the door? And what if he asked me questions about where I heard about the horse?"

"To answer your last question, just say you overheard two men talking about it at the markets, and then say they said the horse was at the Baker Apple Orchard. You were interested in buying a horse, so you took it as a sign that that was the horse you were meant to have."

"Really? Are you sure he's going to believe it?"

"I don't see why not. It sounds quite reasonable to me."

"You Amish are non-violent people, right?"

Cherish giggled and hit his arm. "That's right. He's not going to swing a punch or shoot you."

"Okay." He shoved his hands into his pockets. "It sounds like a bit of fun."

"Thank you, and you'd be really helping everybody out. There's a story attached to the horse, but I won't bore you with that."

"Please do and then I'll know what's at stake."

Cherish told him the story about how the horse was a gift to her mother, and now *Mamm's* brand new husband was taking back that gift.

"Sounds like quite a character, this stepfather of yours."

"Well, yes, he's something alright. He's certainly changed our lives, but not for the better. My mother hasn't said anything, but I'm sure she's upset about the horse."

"Yes, it seems a little weird that someone would decide to sell someone's gift. Especially the gift-giver. Are you sure your mom didn't agree?"

"No. She was shocked when he said he was going to sell the horse."

"When do I start this?"

"Today. He'll be home in a couple of hours. The other thing is Florence and Carter might need to leave the horse here." She looked over her shoulder into the stable block. "Would there be enough room?"

"I think so. They'll have to talk to my mom about that."

"I'll let them know."

He clapped his hands together. "I've got a couple of hours work here and then I'll mosey on over."

"Thank you. Today, just see what he says. Ask to see the horse and then ask him how much. If you have to make the offer, make it low."

"He might be offended if I go too low."

"Don't go that low." Cherish looked over at the heap of manure. "I'll leave you to it."

"Okay. I hope I say everything right."

"You will and don't mention this. It's just between you and me, Florence, and Carter."

"Got it." He grabbed his shovel.

"I'm going. Bye." Cherish walked away, hoping Fairfax would find Levi in a good mood.

CHAPTER NINE

*H*ope rinsed off the newly shelled peas in the metal colander. When she looked out the window and saw Fairfax walking toward the house, she knew he was there to talk to her and her sisters. They'd had such a nice talk the other day.

The only problem was … Levi!

Levi wouldn't appreciate an *Englisher* stopping by.

"I'll be back in a minute," Hope said, as she placed the colander down in the sink. She walked through the kitchen and out the back door, and then Fairfax looked up and saw her.

His face brightened when he saw her. "Hope."

"You remembered."

"Of course I did. Do you remember who I am?"

"I do. You're Fairfax, but I've only got one name to remember, so it's not that hard."

"I only needed to remember yours."

She giggled, knowing he was teasing. Then her cheeks grew hot and all she could do was look down at the ground. "Did you come here to see me?"

"No, I confess that I didn't, but I would like to ask you if you'd have lunch with me sometime."

"Why did you come here?"

"I believe your stepfather is selling a horse and I wanted to talk to him about it."

"Do you want to buy him?"

"I could if the horse suits."

"That would be wonderful. Then he won't go far from home. Everybody loves Wilbur. How do you know about him?"

"I heard someone talking about it." He shifted from one foot to the other. "Do you think you'll be able to meet up with me somewhere tomorrow?"

Her heart raced and then her mouth went dry. She swallowed hard. "I'll be looking for a job all day with my sisters."

"What kind of job are you looking for?"

"Anything, really. I just need a job fast."

He tapped a couple of fingers on his chin. "I do

have an aunt with a B&B. She has a large staff. I could see if she's got anything available."

"Would you? I love B&Bs."

He laughed. "She's a bit grouchy. I'll swing by tomorrow morning and ask her. If she doesn't have anything, I have a couple of friends whose parents have businesses. Normally, it's not what you know but who you know that counts."

"You'd do that for me?"

"I would if you'd have lunch with me."

She laughed. "You're persistent. Do you really have an aunt with a B&B?"

"I do. I seriously do. I wouldn't lie about it. Meet me at twelve o'clock. There's a coffee shop one block from the markets in South Street."

"I think I know the one. It's the one with the green awnings out front?"

"That's the one, and don't bring your sisters. I'm only interested in having lunch with you."

She giggled, loving the attention. "I'll be there, if it's about a job."

"Of course." Fairfax shrugged his shoulders. "It's not a date or anything."

She backed away from him. "I should probably get Levi for you."

"Yes please, and don't forget twelve tomorrow."

"I'll remember." She walked into the house and told her mother someone had come to see Levi about the horse. She knew Levi was somewhere upstairs.

"You can't leave him outside in the cold. Bring him in by the fire," *Mamm* said.

"It's not that cold," said Hope. The truth was that she didn't want her sisters to talk with him. Particularly the boy-crazy, Cherish.

"I'll get *Dat,*" said Bliss as she hurried away.

Five minutes later, the girls and Wilma watched from the kitchen as Matthew led the horse up for Fairfax to look at while Levi talked to him. If Levi was talking so nicely to Fairfax, Cherish knew it meant that he was the only potential buyer.

WHEN FAIRFAX LEFT, the girls went back to cooking the dinner. Cherish ran out of the kitchen to see Levi as soon as he walked into the house alongside Matthew. "Did you sell Wilbur?"

"We're negotiating. I don't think he'll pay the money I want."

"That's good, because we all like Wilbur and don't want you to sell him."

Matthew said, "He liked him, I could tell."

Levi said, "You can like the horse all you want, Cherish, but it will be sold."

"*Jah,* but surely you won't sell him to an *Englisher.* He's too good a horse, *Dat,*" Bliss added.

Drawing his bushy eyebrows together he said, "It doesn't matter where he goes. As long as we get the price we want."

CHAPTER TEN

*F*lorence was walking Spot when she saw Joy hanging around by the edge of the apple trees. Immediately, Florence knew Joy had a problem. She hoped it wasn't second thoughts about Isaac. It was too late for those. When she called out, Joy walked over and they met at the fence that divided their properties.

"How are you, Joy?"

"I'm fine."

"And how's married life?"

Joy shivered with the cold and rubbed her shoulders. "Well, I don't really know. I don't exactly feel like I am married because we don't have our own place."

On hearing that, Florence regretted allowing

Fairfax to rent the cottage that she had intended to offer Isaac and Joy. "Yes, but it won't be long. Besides, living at home's giving you a chance to save up. Let's talk up at the house—if you have the time?"

"*Denke*. I have a little time." Joy slipped through the wires of the fence while Florence helped hold them apart. After Joy patted Spot, they started walking to Florence and Carter's cottage. "I know I should be happy because Isaac and I are married now and that's what I've always wanted, but that's the thing, we can't save money because he's charging us to stay there."

"What do you mean, 'he's charging' you?"

"Levi is. He's charging us just as much as if we were renting a house of our own."

That made Florence annoyed. She wasn't used to seeing Joy look so down. Of all her sisters, she was always the most positive one. It was their father's house, and now his own daughter was being charged to stay there. "I don't see how that's right. Where's the money going?"

Joy shook her head. "I don't know."

"I thought the idea of you staying there was to save money?"

"So did I, but obviously that's not happening now."

"You'll have to move out."

"We're going to. We're moving out as soon as we can."

"That sounds like a good plan. What if you get a caravan and move it onto the orchard?" They walked up the two porch steps and Florence pushed the door open.

"Onto Levi's land?" Joy moved through the door into the warmth and took off her coat.

"It's not technically his land. It's *Mamm's*." Florence took Joy's coat from her and hung it up while Spot walked over to the fire and slumped onto the rug in front of it.

"It might as well be his. It's a good idea, we'd be alone, but he'd still charge us money."

"He wouldn't, would he?" They walked over and sat on the couch.

"I think so."

"You can always use our land if you want. We'll work out a place for it to go. I'm sure it wouldn't be much to rent a caravan."

"I'll look into it. You sure it's okay?"

"I have to ask Carter, of course, but I don't see he'll mind."

"Thank you, Florence. I only hope that Isaac agrees."

"I can't see him disagreeing. It'll give you both the privacy that you need."

"Yes it will."

"When can you ask him?"

Carter walked down the stairs and they both looked up at him. "Ask me what?"

"Joy and Isaac need their own place. I suggested they hire a caravan and they might be able to put it on our land somewhere."

"Of course."

Joy sprang to her feet, ran over and hugged him. "Thanks, Carter. That's so generous, and you too, Florence."

He looked shocked as though he didn't expect any niceness from any of his half-sisters. Florence contained a giggle.

When Joy stepped back, he said, "But I don't know what Wilma would think of that."

"I'll find out. I'll talk with Isaac and if he agrees we'll talk to *Mamm*."

"Can you stay for coffee?" Carter asked.

"No thanks. I'll have to get back to help with the chores."

Florence and Carter walked her to the door.

When she was a fair distance from the house, they closed the door and faced one another.

"Did you see that?" he asked.

"I know, I saw."

"Normally they completely ignore me. They all seem a bit cold. Except for Cherish, and now Joy. I think she likes me."

Florence giggled. "They all like you. It was quite an adjustment for them to make when they found out who you were. They had no idea of your existence."

He nodded. "I know that. Maybe if they're coming around, so will Wilma—eventually."

Florence sighed. "I think I'll make us some coffee. Want some?"

Carter followed her through to the kitchen. "You don't think she'll come around?"

"Nope. But I hope she will..."

"Sit, I'll make the coffee."

She sat on the kitchen stool. "Thanks. It sounds like Joy and Isaac aren't having a good time of it."

"Was it that bad when you were living there?"

"Not really. If it was, I didn't notice."

Slowly, he nodded. "I hope things work out for Joy and Isaac. They must be going through a hard time right now. That Levi sounds like a tyrant."

"I can't work it out. He was always so quiet and seemed so generous."

"Not anymore by the sounds of it. Now that he's got what he wanted, it sounds like he's turned into a different person."

"I can't believe he's making all the girls work five days a week or he won't feed them. They have to give him all their money and he's making Wilma do all the household things and she's not used to it. She must be exhausted."

"Forgive me, but I can't find it in my heart to feel sorry for Wilma."

She looked at him and didn't know what to say. They were both bitter over the things that Wilma had done. "It's not good to feel resentful."

He pressed the button and the coffee began to fill the mug. "Yeah, I know, but I'm not going to start feeling guilty over my feelings." He turned around to face her. "Isn't guilt another bad emotion?"

Reaching out her hand, she said, "Just give me the coffee."

CHAPTER ELEVEN

*H*ope had managed to get away from her sisters by telling them she had a lead for a job. She left them at the markets and walked to the café with her heart nearly pumping out of her chest. Talking to boys made her nervous and knowing that he liked her made her even more nervous.

As she walked past the window of the café, she saw him sitting, waiting. His hair was tousled, and he wore a light blue long-sleeved shirt.

You can do this, she told herself as she walked through the door. When she looked over at him, she saw him grinning at her.

Breathlessly, Hope sat down in front of Fairfax. "I've only got an hour. I had to tell them I was coming for a job interview. I don't want to be lying. Do you have news about a job?"

He smiled at her. "Hello."

She giggled. "Hello. I'm sorry. It's just that I don't like deceiving people."

"Fair point. You'll be happy to know then that my aunt does have a job opening."

"Really?" She stared at him in disbelief. Up until now, she'd thought that this was just a ruse to get her to come to lunch. "Are you kidding me right now?"

He laughed, "I wouldn't do that. But I don't know if you want the job as a cleaner?"

"Cleaning, that would be perfect. Yes."

"I know it's not the most exciting job in the world."

"It's perfect."

"I told her you'd come and see her this afternoon, if that's alright."

"That would be perfect. Where is it?"

He gave her the address.

"That's not far from home. I could probably walk there if I had to."

He shook his head. "It's way too far to walk. I could take you."

"I couldn't bother you and besides that, I don't

think I'll be allowed. Oh, what am I talking about? I haven't even got the job yet."

"I'm sure you'll get it. I recommended you."

"And what's your aunt's name?"

"Jane Jenkins."

"Jane Jenkins. That's an easy name to remember. Your name, Jenkins and her name starts with a J."

He smiled at her and passed over a menu.

She looked up and down the menu too nervous to eat. "I'm not very hungry."

"Me neither. What about we just order pizza to share?"

"Sounds good." After they placed the order, she asked him what happened about the horse.

"I made him an offer and he refused it. I said I'd think about whether I could offer more, and I'd come back."

"I'm so pleased you like Wilbur. What do you plan to do with him?"

"My mother likes horses and she does show jumping. You should see all her ribbons and trophies. The house is full of them."

"So … what will you do with Wilbur?"

"Maybe Mom might like to try harness racing."

"You're buying him for your Mom?"

"No."

Hope couldn't work out what he was talking about, and why he wanted the horse. "I think his racing days would be behind him. I don't think he'd be suited to a life like that."

"Then I won't race him. Not if it makes you upset."

Her face relaxed into a smile.

"That's better." He placed his elbows onto the table and rested his chin on his hands and stared at her. "You have the most unusual color eyes."

"No, I don't. They're just eyes."

He laughed. "You should learn to take a compliment. I'll show you. Say something nice about me."

"Um, nice shirt."

"Thank you. I washed it yesterday so it wouldn't stink when I got here today."

She giggled. "Then what am I supposed to say, 'I washed my eyes?'"

"You could say that … no, forget it. Ignore me. Say whatever you want and it's perfectly okay."

Hope figured a change of subject was needed. "Shall I go to your aunt's this afternoon?"

"Yes, she's expecting you sometime today."

"Oh good. I can't thank you enough."

The waitress brought their pizza and their sodas. Hope was too nervous to eat, but she managed a couple of slices in between chatting to Fairfax.

"My sisters are waiting. Thanks for the meal and for arranging the interview with your aunt."

"My pleasure, and maybe I'll see you again sometime?"

"I hope so."

"The weekend?"

"Um, I don't know. It depends on this interview, doesn't it? I might be working on Saturday."

"Yes of course. I'm sure we'll see each other soon."

"I'm sure." After they exchanged smiles, Hope hurried away. Maybe she should've been more encouraging and made a proper time for them to meet again. Had she brushed him away? Did he now think she wasn't interested? When she saw the buggy, she decided it was best not to give Fairfax encouragement. It was okay to be friendly, but she couldn't let herself be drawn in by his good looks and his cheerful personality.

WITH HER SISTERS tired of job searching and ready to go home. Hope told them she had one more stop to make. She drove to the bed and breakfast and told the others to wait in the buggy.

Hope then stepped through the door of the B&B. Her feet immediately sank into the thick red-swirl patterned carpet. On the antique carved wooden desk in front of her sat a bowl full of pink roses. Hope couldn't resist walking up to smell her favorite flowers and filling her lungs with the sweet fragrance.

There was a sign with a hand pointing and it said, *Ring the Bell.*

When she looked everywhere and there was no bell, she called out, "Hello?" She walked into the hallway and soon found herself in a large living area with many doorways off from it. There was one door open, so she moved toward it. "Hello?"

To her surprise it was a kitchen, galley style, long and rectangular and a woman stood at the end.

"Hello," she said again, wondering if this was Fairfax's aunt.

A flustered looking woman looked up at her and slammed the oven door shut,

The woman then fixed a smile on her face. "Yes?"

"It's just that I'm looking for a job and I thought you might have something here. Um, do you know Fairfax?"

"You're Hope?"

"That's right."

The woman looked her up and down. "He never mentioned his new girlfriend was Amish. We do have a position for a cleaner. Our main cleaner just left with no notice. Do you clean?"

Hope couldn't believe her ears for two reasons. He'd called her his girlfriend? And, she did have a job. When the woman continued to stare at her, Hope realized she was waiting for a reply. "I do, I clean every day."

"Good." The woman leaned on the counter. "Do you know how to make beds properly?"

"I've been shown by someone who used to work in a hotel."

"Is that so?"

"Yes. She showed me how to fold and tuck in the corners and I even know how to make all kinds of decorations out of hand towels and washcloths."

"That won't be necessary. Sounds like you have the skills." She looked her up and down for a second time. "When can you start?"

"Any time. I don't have a job. Not even a part-time one."

"Why don't you have a job?"

"I've just started looking."

"Well, you're in luck. I'll start you right out from tomorrow and we'll see how we both get along. How does that sound?"

"That sounds just fine. Thank you very much. What do I have to do, do I have to wear anything special?"

"Just wear clothes that you can clean in. And be here at seven sharp."

"Seven. I can do that. Until when?"

"Two. I suppose you don't work Sundays?"

"I don't."

"Can you do Monday through Saturday?"

"Yes. I can."

"You're an answer to prayer. And, I should ask your full name. I only know your first name."

"Hope Baker."

"Good afternoon, Hope Baker, I'm Jane Jenkins." She put out her hand. "Congratulations to you for your new job and congratulations to me for finding a cleaner so soon after the last one left."

Hope smiled, pleased that the woman seemed nice. Hope hurried back to the buggy. "I've got a job."

The others stared at her.

"Really?"

"I thought you were in there for a long time," said Bliss.

"Long enough to get myself the job. I can't believe it. I start at seven tomorrow morning."

"I'm so excited for you," said Favor. "I was praying for you the whole time you were in there."

"Denke." Hope picked up the reins and headed toward home.

Bliss leaned over from the back seat. *"Dat* will be so pleased that you got a job, Hope."

"Jah he will, but there might be more pressure on all of you."

"Nee," Bliss said. "It should take the pressure off the rest of us. Because one wage will be coming into the family."

Hope didn't like to be reminded that all her wages would be taken from her and she would get a meager allowance in return. That took the excitement out of getting the job.

When they got home, Favor helped Hope practice making beds fast. She guessed that she would have to do everything quickly and efficiently so her boss would be happy with her. She was sure she was getting faster and faster even though the timer they borrowed from their mother denied it.

FLORENCE AND CARTER had just finished their dinner when they heard someone walk up the steps to their front door. Carter opened the door and then Florence heard Fairfax's voice.

"Come in," Carter said. "Would you like a cup of tea or anything?"

"No thanks, this is just a quick visit."

"About the horse?" Carter asked motioning to him to move through to the living room.

He saw Florence sitting on the couch. "Hi Florence."

"Hi there."

When they were all seated, he answered Carter. "That's right. I've come about the horse. I've got no idea what to offer and I haven't seen Cherish lately. She gave me no clear indication of what to pay for the horse."

Carter held his hands up in front of him. "This is not my area of expertise at all. I'm a city boy. I know nothing about the country, livestock and such."

Florence asked, "Do you have any idea how much he wants?"

"Not really, he didn't give me much idea at all. I

think he wants more than a couple of thousand dollars."

"Yes, I think he's quite a valuable horse," agreed Florence.

"We could go up to eight," Carter said.

Florence spluttered. "Eight, just for a horse that we're going to keep as a pet?"

"Yes. That's what you want, isn't it?"

"I do, but it's a lot of money and it's kind of like money down the drain since we have to spend so much money on getting the orchard prepared. The drainage itself is going to cost a small fortune."

"We can't disappoint those bonnet sisters of yours. They're relying on us."

Fairfax laughed and repeated, "Bonnet sisters, eh?"

Florence looked at Carter, wishing he hadn't said that to Fairfax because she didn't want her sisters to be known around town as the bonnet sisters. They were the Baker sisters, that's what their name was, not the bonnet sisters.

He saw Florence looking at him and he shrugged his shoulders. "Sorry, it's a habit. And you know how hard habits are to break."

"Hmm."

"I think I might've gotten Hope a job today."

"Really?" Florence was pleased about that. She'd heard the girls were under terrible pressure to find work. The notion was crazy. Their stepfather's idea was that the orchard would support them all. Done properly, it could've done so, especially with all the goods they could've baked and the cider they could've made. All that had fallen by the wayside because Levi was too short-sighted and Wilma was too easily led. "What job?" she asked.

"My aunt has a bed and breakfast and she's looking for a cleaner, so that is good news."

"She'd be very happy about that. I can't wait to find out if she got it."

"Me too."

EVERYONE INCLUDING her mother advised Hope that it would be best to wait to tell Levi her news when they were gathered around the dining table for the evening meal.

When they were seated and had all filled their plates with the crispy roasted chicken, and vegetables, *Mamm* prompted, "Hope, what did you have to tell Levi?"

Levi stopped chewing and looked over at her.

Hope looked back at him. "You know how we all went out looking for jobs today?"

"*Jah,* did one of you find work?"

"I did."

He smiled. It was rare for Levi to smile and Hope was pleased that she was the cause of it.

"*Wunderbaar,* Hope. When do you start?"

"Tomorrow morning. I have to be there at seven. I'm cleaning at the bed and breakfast down at the end of Pebbles Lane."

Levi nodded. "I know the one. How are you going to get there?"

Hope's heart raced when she realized from his comment that he wasn't going to allow her to take one of the buggies. "I thought I would take the buggy."

He shook his head. "We have to learn to do with less. I will take one buggy tomorrow and then the girls will have to take the other out while they're looking for jobs."

"That's easily solved. Someone can take me to work and pick me up."

He shook his head. "It's too much work for the horses. You can ride your bike."

"I don't have one. *Mamm* never allowed us to have bikes because she said they were dangerous."

"You can ride Bliss's bike. Now that you're older I'm sure your *mudder* won't mind you riding a bike."

"Of course. Ride my bike any time you want, Hope."

Hope felt a headache coming on. Why wasn't anything ever simple? She thought all her problems would be solved when she found a job. Now she had another hurdle to jump. "I can't ride a bike. Otherwise, that would be a good solution."

"After dinner, Bliss can teach you."

"Will I be able to learn in time for tomorrow?"

"There's nothing to it," he said.

Hope had heard that line before, with unhappy results. She had a bad feeling, but tried to ignore it and kept eating her dinner.

CHAPTER TWELVE

*A*fter the dinner washing up was done, everybody gathered on the porch watching Hope attempt to ride the bike. Matthew was doing his best to instruct her. The darkness of night was illuminated by the same flood lights that had lit Wilma and Levi's wedding weeks before.

There were many spills and many tears, but two hours later, Hope was riding the bike with Matthew running alongside in case she fell. "I can do it; I can do it!"

Levi stood and leaned on the porch railing as he watched. "I knew you could do it."

"Now, let us all get in out of the cold. Put the bike away, Hope. I'll make us all some hot chocolate to warm us."

Hope wheeled the bike into the barn with Matthew on the other side of the bike.

"You did real good, Hope."

"*Denke*. I hope I don't forget how to ride it by morning."

"They say once you learn to ride a bike, you never forget."

"That's good to hear. I hope it's true." She leaned the bike against the wall and walked out of the barn. When she saw he wasn't following, she turned around. "Coming?"

He took a step toward her. "Hope, would you ever be interested in a guy like me?"

In the semi-darkness, she stood there not knowing what to say. Sure, he was nice enough, but she didn't love him. If she said no, he'd be shattered, but if she said yes, that would give him false hope. "Matthew, just because your two brothers married my two older sisters, that doesn't mean you and I will be a good idea."

"That's not what I'm doing. That'd be pretty silly. Do you think I'm a silly kind of guy?"

Now the whole thing was even more awkward. She felt like hitting herself in the head for saying something so dumb, but she knew many people were thinking it would be nice if Matthew married a Baker girl. "Right now, I'm not thinking of liking anyone."

"Yeah, but if you were?"

"It's not a fair question. Let's go inside. They're making hot chocolate and I'd daresay *Mamm* will find some marshmallows too." She walked ahead of him not waiting. First Fairfax and now Matthew... It was nice to have some male attention, but neither of them felt right.

Once they were all gathered around the fire sipping hot drinks, there was a knock on their door.

"Just when we were about to start our reading," Levi said. "Go see who it is, Joy."

"Perhaps, they'd like to join us, *Dat*," said Bliss.

"You might be right." Levi smiled at his daughter while Joy opened the door.

Hope heard a male voice. It was Fairfax and he was telling Joy he was there to talk with Levi about the horse.

Levi heard too and went to the door. He suggested they talk in the kitchen. Fairfax walked into the house and gave everyone a smile and a wave before he followed Levi into the kitchen.

"He's buying Wilbur by the sounds," Wilma whispered to everyone.

"That's good, Wilbur won't be going far away," Cherish said.

Mamm made no comment.

Half an hour later, the two men emerged from the kitchen. Fairfax then walked to the door, gave everyone a polite wave and then he and Levi shook hands at the doorway. "I'll bring the cash tomorrow," he told Levi when he stood at the door.

"I'll have the horse ready."

"Thanks."

Fairfax hadn't even looked directly at Hope when he waved at the family those two times. It was just as well because she didn't want anyone to guess that they liked one another.

Levi closed the door looking pleased with himself. When he walked back to the living room, he sat down. "I sold him for a good price."

No one said a word. Then he picked up his mug and looked into it. "Wilma, it's gone cold. Get me another."

Wilma got up and looked around. "Anyone else want another?"

"I'm fine, *denke,* Mrs. Baker," said Matthew.

"You sit, I'll get it, *Mamm,*" said Favor.

"*Nee,* Favor. We can all get ready for our Bible reading."

"That's just great!" said Cherish sarcastically.

"You're not interested in *Gott's* word?"

"I am, but we were all having a good time with our marshmallows and our hot chocolate just sitting around talking. We can't talk with a Bible reading. Doesn't the Bible say there's a time for everything? A time to live, a time to die, a time to plant, a time to sow?"

Levi chuckled. *"Gut,* Cherish. That's where we shall begin our reading from. Ecclesiastes. It seems you're fond of it so you can read it out for all of us."

"Jah, and then you'll be talking," Bliss cackled loudly.

It was all Cherish could do to hold her tongue. "Okay, I'd love to." She wouldn't let Levi see she was upset.

Bliss stood up, got her father's Bible from the table in the corner, and then walked over and handed it to Cherish. "Shall I find Ecclesiastes for you?"

Cherish took the Bible from her. "I know where it is, *denke."*

CHAPTER THIRTEEN

*H*ope was excited for her first day at work. After her mother made her a quick breakfast, she dressed and then headed out to the barn to get the bike. When she wheeled it out, Matthew was there, waiting.

"Just remember what you learned last night," he told her.

Hope appreciated his encouragement and threw one leg over and sat on the bike while her tiptoes met the ground. *"Denke.* I think I'll be okay."

"Have a go."

With one foot, she turned the pedal and then took the other foot off the ground. After she wobbled for a moment, she gained her balance.

"That's it, Hope, keep on, keeping on going."

Hope giggled with excitement as Matthew ran beside her just the same as he had done the previous night. "I'm doing it."

"Go." He stopped and she continued on her way down the driveway.

When she reached the road, she felt her leg muscles straining. She'd used them too much the night before.

Not brave enough to make the left turn, she stopped her bike, turned it and then got back on. Off she pedaled into the cold morning with wind gusting against her face. She looked up at the gray sky and wasn't totally sure that it wouldn't rain any minute. It would be a bad impression if she arrived on the first day of work soaking wet through to the skin.

When she was half a mile from her house, she got into the rhythm of things and started feeling better. Riding the bike wasn't so bad. It was really kind of fun. When she heard a vehicle coming up behind her, she glanced around and the handlebars turned at the same time. When she turned them back to keep to the side of the road, she oversteered and lost control completely.

The truck's horn sounded and then she saw the large rock too late. She couldn't avoid it and it brought the bike to a complete halt. While the bike stopped, she kept going over the top of the handle-bars, hitting the ground hard.

The pickup pulled up ahead of her.

Hope was winded, not sure how hurt she was or if she'd broken something. She decided nothing was broken as there wasn't any severe pain. Then she felt strong hands lift her to her feet. It was Fairfax.

"That was a good trick. Do you think you could do that again?"

She realized the only things hurt were a couple of grazed palms and her pride.

The tears flowed without her being able to control them.

She looked up at him and then dusted off her grazed hands.

"I'm sorry for laughing. I didn't know you were hurt."

With the back of her hand, she wiped her eyes. "I'm not. I'm okay."

His gaze traveled to the bike and he leaned over and picked it up. "The frame's a bit bent."

"Oh no! I'm going to get into the worst trouble. It's not even my bike."

He examined her curiously. "You're going to get into trouble for having an accident?"

"Yes. Can it be unbent? It's my new stepsister's bike. I just know I'll get into trouble."

He scratched his head. "That's not good. And it was my fault coming up behind you, scaring you."

"No, it wasn't your fault. I can't ride a bike, obviously."

"I startled you. I only meant to say hello."

"It wasn't you, it was me."

"There's no use going back and forth over whose fault it was. I'll tell you what, why don't I drive you there and then I'll fix the bike and collect you when you finish work?"

"You could fix it?"

"I don't see why not. I've done this kind of thing before."

"That would be wonderful."

He leaned over and picked up the bike with one hand and walked to his pickup truck and placed it in the back. She marveled at how strong he was, being able to pick up the bike with one hand like that. He turned around and smiled at her. "Jump in."

As soon as she was in the truck he got in the driver's seat.

He pulled out onto the road. "I've never seen you ride a bike before."

"That's because it's the first time. I have been forced to ride the bike by my stepfather."

"That doesn't sound like much fun."

"It's not much fun for me because I only learned to ride last night."

"Looks to me like you could do with a few more lessons."

"I think so."

"What are you doing riding in this weather, anyway?"

"It's a long story. I can tell you it wasn't my idea."

When they arrived in the parking lot, he turned off his engine, "What time do you finish?"

"She said it would be two o'clock."

"Good luck on your first day."

"Thank you. I've been practicing making beds."

"I hope your hands will be okay."

She looked down at them. "They're okay."

When she put her hand on the door handle, he asked, "If you want some extra money, maybe you could come clean my cottage."

She put one foot on the gravel. "I don't think you'd be able to afford me."

He raised his hands in the air as though he was giving up.

She giggled. "I do appreciate your help. I'll clean for you in exchange for fixing the bike."

"*Nee*. I don't need payment for that. I've got to collect my horse today, but I'll be able to do everything in time to see you here at two."

"Are you sure?"

"Yeah, no sweat."

She got out and as she listened to the pickup truck drive away from her, she looked down at her clothes. And then she brushed some more dirt off the bottom of her apron.

CHAPTER FOURTEEN

Florence looked out the window when she heard a truck. It was a white pickup truck.

"Carter, Fairfax is here."

Carter made his way down the stairs and opened the door before Fairfax reached it.

"Ah, hullo, do you have news for us?"

The two men shook hands and then Fairfax nodded hello to Florence, who was standing behind Carter.

"I do. We agreed on the price. We got the horse for two and a half."

"Is that all?" Carter said.

"That's what we ended up agreeing on."

Florence was concerned. It meant that Levi

wasn't a good businessman and he was running the orchard.

"I don't have that much cash on me. I'll have to make a trip to the bank."

Fairfax rubbed his chin. "Could you do that soon? I want to give him the money and get the horse before he changes his mind."

"Yes, good idea," Florence said.

"What if I drive you to the bank and bring you back here and then I'll continue on to get the horse.?" Fairfax suggested.

"That sounds like a good idea." Carter looked at Florence "Do you want to come too and we'll take our car?"

"No, I've got plenty here to keep me occupied."

"Okay, I'll be back soon." He gave Florence a quick kiss on the cheek and then he left with Fairfax.

Florence closed the door. She'd known from the first time she'd seen Fairfax that there was something nice about him. He had seemed like someone who could be trusted and she was glad her judgment had been confirmed.

IT WAS late-morning and Cherish was coming to the end of pinning out the washing when she saw

Fairfax walking toward her. She finished pinning the last sheet and waved him over.

"You picking up the horse today?" she asked.

"I am."

"That's good. Gave you the money then, did they?"

"That's right."

"Thanks for doing this."

"Of course. I'm always willing to help out."

"That's good to know. I'll keep that in mind. I hate to see him go but at least I know he's going to a good home. I don't think Wilma will want to visit him but she'll feel better knowing he's right next door."

"How about you get your stepfather for me and tell him I'm here?"

"Sure." As she walked into the house to get Levi, she was a little bewildered that her flirting and girlish giggles didn't work on Fairfax like they seemed to on every other young man. Was she losing her touch? "Levi!" she called out when she got to the kitchen. When there was no answer, she walked into the living area and saw him sitting by the fire reading the paper.

He looked up at her. *"Jah?"*

"The neighbor's here for the horse."

A smile lit up his face and he folded the paper in two before he placed it down on the coffee table in front of him. Then he pushed himself to his feet. "Good. I'm glad he didn't change his mind. It's hard to know with … you can't always trust an *Englisher*."

"He seems pretty trustworthy to me."

Levi didn't make a comment. He walked past her and out the front door.

Favor and Joy came down from upstairs. "He's come to get the horse?" Joy asked.

"*Jah.* Where's *Mamm?*"

"I'll get her." Favor ran back upstairs.

When Wilma joined them, they made their way out of the house to watch. Levi already had a rope around the horse's neck and he passed it over to Fairfax. With one hand Fairfax took hold of the rope, and with the other, he handed Levi a fistful of notes. Levi took the money with two hands and then quickly counted it by thumbing through it. Then the two men shook hands.

"Go and say goodbye to the horse, *Mamm,*" Favor said.

"*Nee,* I'm saying goodbye from here," she said.

"Suit yourself," said Cherish as she headed toward the horse. "Wait up," she called out to Fairfax.

He stopped walking and Cherish patted Wilbur on the neck. "Goodbye. You've been a very good horse."

The horse pushed her with his nose.

Fairfax looked up to see everyone watching him. "Well, I'll see y'all later." He gave Levi a nod and then waved at the women on the porch before he walked down the driveway.

Levi then walked inside, and said to Wilma as he passed, "I'm going to put this money in the family banking account."

"Oh good. Does that mean it's my money too?" asked Cherish.

"It's all of our money," Levi said, "but only your *mudder* or I can draw it out."

"I knew it was too good to be true," she muttered.

He stared at her. "Why aren't you out looking for a job?"

"Favor and I are just going out now, aren't we, Favor?"

"*Gut,*" Levi said. "I'll come with you and put the money in the bank."

"Won't you be bored sitting in the buggy while we stop in at all the different places?"

He rubbed his beard. "Maybe I'll just do it myself tomorrow."

"Okay." Cherish was relieved. She loved traveling into town and back with her sisters, talking about silly things, laughing and gossiping. She knew her sisters wouldn't judge her for whatever she said, but around Levi she had to watch every little word.

CHAPTER FIFTEEN

*H*ope looked up at the clock on the kitchen wall. It was already after two. She finished up what she was doing and headed to the kitchen to find her boss.

"There you are, Hope. You can go if you like. You don't need to ask me. Once you see it's two you can head out the door."

"Okay. Thank you."

"Payday is Friday."

"Do I get paid this Friday even though I haven't worked a full week?"

"You'll get paid for the days you worked."

She headed out the door and saw the white pickup truck immediately. Fairfax had his head down and didn't look up at her. What if he hadn't been able to fix the bike? What punishment would she get from Levi, and would Bliss carry on and cry?

Once she was level with the driver's door, she saw he was doing something on his cell. She knocked on the door and he jumped. Then he smiled and opened his door.

"Sorry to keep you waiting."

"No problem."

"Were you able to fix the bike?"

"Yes, it's all fixed, but why don't I drive you home?"

"Um …" She wondered what Levi would think of that. "I don't think I'll be allowed. I better just ride the bike thanks."

"Aw, come on. Let me take you."

Then she heard a buggy and turned around. It was too far to see who the driver was, but it was one of her family's horses and she was certain the lone driver was Matthew. He was in love with her, so the last thing she wanted was to give him encouragement by going with him. Without a word, she quickly moved to the other side and jumped in. "Quick, drive."

When he drove away, Fairfax looked in the rearview mirror. "Who was that?"

"Matthew. He's staying with my parents. His two brothers are married to two of my sisters."

"Ah, and he wants to make it a trifecta?"

"Exactly! That's what I said."

"Did you know he was coming?"

"Not at all." She shook her head.

"Maybe he wasn't."

"He must've been because there's not much else on this road. It doesn't really go anywhere."

Fairfax glanced over at her. "I hope you're not going to get into trouble now."

"I'm getting tired of it."

He grinned at her. "Tired of what?"

"I'm getting tired of my stepfather with all his new rules."

"What kind of rules?"

"I don't know, but he's the outsider. I don't know why things can't just remain how they were before he came into the family."

"Do you think that's possible?"

"Most definitely." When they got close to home, she said, "I'm so not looking forward to going home."

"Come back to my place for a while. I'll show you my cottage."

"So, they allowed you to lease it? You came to

our place the day you were going to ask Florence and Carter."

"Yes, I remember. I used my charms. No one can resist my charms." He glanced over at her and smiled. "What do you say, will you come back and see my place?"

"I guess so, thank you." Anything would be better than going back home. "It's so crowded there now. There were just the four of us and my stepfather and his daughter have moved in. It's hectic and quite stressful." It felt good to have someone interested in her. He was her own special person, focused only on her. Now she understood why her older married sisters were so happy.

"I'm really pleased you fell off your bike."

She twisted her whole body to stare at him. "And why is that?"

"I was wondering how I could get to talk to you. It seemed impossible."

He glanced over at her and she felt her cheeks warm and then she looked away from him.

"I was hoping … I shouldn't say it."

"Hoping what? Say it."

"Would you go out one time on a proper date?"

"Oh, this is fairly unexpected."

"It will get you away from that family of yours."

"That's true, but... What did you have in mind?"

"I don't know, I'll think of something."

"I haven't said yes yet. I thought you liked my older sister?"

"No, she was a bit serious for me. I like girls who are more fun-loving."

"I'm not very fun. Cherish is the sister who is the fun-loving one. She's a real risk-taker."

"Which one was that?"

"Cherish. She's the youngest one."

"I wouldn't know. I only have eyes for you."

She couldn't keep the smile from her face. "Is that right?"

"Of course."

"Honesty is very important to me."

"Just as well I'm an honest type of guy." They turned into his driveway and then drove past his parents' house. As he was driving past one of the outbuildings, his mother stepped out and waved them down.

"Hi, Mom."

"I've just got a call that your furniture is arriving tomorrow at ten."

"I wonder why they didn't call me."

"They said it went to your messages."

"The service around here is terrible, I've been told," Hope said.

His mother crouched down and looked over at her. "Cherish, I didn't see you there. It's nice to see you again."

Before Hope could say anything, he said, "Thanks, Mom. Talk later." He accelerated toward his house and then stopped the truck. Hope opened the door very quickly. She could see what was going on here. He was a liar.

CHAPTER SIXTEEN

"*W*ait up, Hope."

She looked up at him, disappointed. "Cherish has been here? I thought you only liked me. That's what you just said only one minute ago."

"I know and it's true. I have no idea why she thought you were Cherish."

"It's obvious. You've had *her* here at your house."

His eyes opened wide. "I haven't. Well, she was here but I didn't invite her."

She walked around to the back and then tried to get her bike out of the truck. Before she got it off completely, he helped her.

"I hope you believe me."

"Of course I don't. I'm not stupid." She stared

into his eyes. "Why didn't you tell me." She hitched her dress up slightly and threw her leg over the other side of the bike. "Thank you again for fixing the bike."

"Hope, don't leave like this. Come with me and we'll ask my mother why she called you Cherish. I don't know how she could've even met her."

"No, that's not the kind of thing I want to do."

"I still don't know how my mother knows her. As you can see, she doesn't know her well if she thought you were Cherish."

"Goodbye, Fairfax." The bike wobbled as she rode off, but she managed to balance it.

When she had to drive past his mother, Mrs. Jenkins smiled and waved. Hope gave a quick nod and kept pedaling. She was so upset she gave no thought to how she was riding. There was no reason Cherish would know Mrs. Jenkins unless she'd been introduced by Fairfax.

Fairfax wasn't telling her the truth and Cherish was so secretive that Hope would never find out what was going on.

In the freezing winter air, the tears froze on her face and clung to her cheeks. She had felt special when he said he liked her and only her. She never had anyone special and it had felt good while it'd lasted.

When she was riding up the driveway to her house, she knew she wasn't ready to talk with anyone. Then she saw Matthew tending his horse in the paddock, and she changed her mind. She stopped and got off the bike, and wheeled it the rest of the way.

She didn't mind when he strode over. "You got home safely. I was worried. I saw you drive off in a pickup truck. Are you okay?"

"Yes, I fell off the bike and the people from the neighboring property drove me home."

He put his hands on her shoulders and looked at her strangely making her think her eyes must've been red. "I'm okay. The bike is okay too."

"I'm so pleased you weren't hurt."

He took the bike and started wheeling it into the barn.

Maybe she'd been too hasty when it came to disregarding Matthew as a prospective boyfriend.

"It all looks like it's in good working order," he said to her looking over his shoulder.

She caught up with him. "Thank you for putting the bike away, but I could've done it."

"Sure. I'd do anything for you Hope, anything.

You should know the only reason I stayed on here is to get to know you better."

Now she felt bad for not returning those feelings. "The only reason?"

"Yes. It's the only reason."

She'd always thought of Matthew as just a kid, now she was starting to appreciate him, seeing him in a new light. He would've been raised with the same values and beliefs as hers, so he'd never lie to her like Fairfax had.

Once they were inside the barn, he leaned the bike against the wall. "Can

we sit down here for a while and talk?"

"Okay."

He pulled out hay bales for them to sit on.

"How was work?"

"A lot better than I thought it would be."

"Do you work with many others?"

She was pleased he was talking about things other than the fact that he liked her. "Besides the boss, there was one other lady who worked in the kitchen."

"And what do you do exactly?"

"Clean the rooms. Jane said it's not very busy this time of year. She's only got two rooms out of the ten occupied."

"I've often thought about having a bed and break-fast when I get older."

"Have you ever even had a job?"

"Not a paid one. I've done loads of work for friends and family."

"That's nice."

"What I really want to do is buy and sell things."

"What kind of things?" Just talking to him made her feel better.

"Anything."

"Mark's got a saddlery store. Do you mean like that?"

"*Jah,* I'd like to work for myself. I haven't found my thing yet."

"There's plenty of time."

"Not too much time. The main thing I want to do is make a lot of money so I can support a large family. I love children."

"You must be pleased about your two brothers having children."

"No, I'm madly jealous."

She laughed.

"I guess I am happy for them, but it makes my desire for children all the more stronger. How about you?"

"I guess I'll have some someday. I'm not so much in a rush. How many children do you want?"

"As many as *Gott* will give us."

She giggled again and covered her mouth with her fingertips.

"I mean give me and the woman I end up marrying."

"I know. I thought that's what you meant."

"Wouldn't it be neat if maybe we got married?"

Now she was really uncomfortable. He didn't know what it was to be subtle. "Why, because your two brothers are married to my sisters? There has to be more of a basis for marriage than that, don't you think?"

He smiled. "It'd be a good start."

Talking to him made her start to feel a little better after what had happened with Fairfax.

"I'm only saying these things because I go home soon. Will you spend the day with me on Saturday?"

Being with him would take her mind off Fairfax. *"Jah,* I will, but I work until two, so after I get home. As long as you know that I can't see things going any further than just friends."

"I can deal with that. Friends is good."

"Okay then. I'll look forward to it." She was shocked when she heard the words come out of her mouth, but there was little else to do on Saturday afternoon and any excuse to get out of the house would've been a good excuse. "If ... my sisters will do my chores for me on Saturday."

"I'm sure they will. Do you want me to ask them?"

"*Nee*, I will."

"Thank you, Hope. We will have a good time."

She stood up and smoothed her dress. "I suppose we should go inside now."

He rose to his feet and touched her arm. "Do you feel a bit better?"

"What's going on in here?" a large voice boomed. They turned around to see Levi in the doorway of the barn, hands on hips and looking none too happy.

"We were just talking," Matthew said.

He eyed them both suspiciously. "Just talking, eh?"

"That's right. Hope has agreed to go out with me on Saturday before I leave."

"I don't think that's a very good idea, Matthew. From what I've just seen you can stay the rest of the time at Ada's house."

"Believe me, there was nothing going on, Mr. Baker."

"'Baker?'" His dark eyebrows lowered.

"Nee, it's Mr. Brunner. I'm sorry." Matthew looked down. "I get confused because the girls are Bakers."

"Go inside, pack your things, and I'll take you there right now."

Hope stepped forward. "Is that really necessary?"

"It's not your place to say anything, Hope. You can cancel your plans for Saturday."

"We weren't doing anything wrong. We were just talking. Sitting right there on those hay bales." She turned around and pointed to them.

"You were in here for a long time. I saw you both going in and you didn't come out."

It was useless. Hope didn't know what to do. When Matthew started walking away, she said, "Can't he stay until after dinner?"

Levi just turned to Matthew. "Get your things, Matthew."

"Yes, Mr. Brunner."

Hope caught up with Matthew and they walked to the house side by side. "I'm so sorry, Matthew. I would've loved to have gone out with you Saturday and gotten to know you a little bit better."

"That's okay. Perhaps I should go home. There's no point sticking around now. Will you write to me?"

"Of course I will."

When he went upstairs to get his things, Hope went into the kitchen to tell everyone what had happened, but she didn't get a chance because Levi followed her in.

"I'm taking Matthew to Ada's house. He can't stay here any longer. I found him and Hope in the barn together, alone."

"We weren't doing anything," said Hope.

"That's how these things start off," he said.

Hope walked out of the room not wanting to hear any more. She sat down in the living room and then Cherish came out of the kitchen and sat next to her. Cherish was the last person she wanted to talk with.

"What's going on?" asked Cherish.

"Nothing. We were just talking and then Levi thought we were doing something we shouldn't. We were only in there for ten minutes at the most."

Favor sat down with them. "Is this what our life is going to be like now until we leave home? Living under Levi's laws?"

Cherish sniggered "'Levi's laws.' Yeah, who knew he was going to be like this? He's so unreasonable and he won't even believe us."

"He hates us," whispered Favor.

Bliss walked out from the kitchen and sat down

with them. "That's too bad about Matthew leaving, isn't it?"

The other girls nodded. They couldn't continue the conversation in front of Levi's daughter. She already knew they weren't happy with him over selling the horse.

CHAPTER SEVENTEEN

On Monday morning, Cherish was surprised when she set a breakfast plate in front of Levi and he pushed it away from him. "Is there something wrong with it?" she asked. "I made it just the way you like it."

"I asked Wilma to make it for me."

Cherish looked across at her mother who was seated opposite him. "But it's already there. It's made."

Levi looked up at her. "But it's not been made by Wilma."

Cherish didn't know what to do, so she sat down with her own breakfast. Meanwhile, *Mamm* had her head lowered and hadn't moved off her chair.

He stared at Wilma. "Well? I'd like my breakfast now."

She pushed his discarded breakfast back over to him. "And there it is."

He pushed the food away. "I want my *fraa* to make my breakfast."

"It's a waste of food. Who is going to eat that?"

"I'll give it to the dogs."

"*Nee*. It's good food and I won't see it go to waste. Eat it." She pushed the food back to him once more.

He stood up and then walked over to her, lifted her by the arm and pulled her towards the oven. "Cook the food."

Cherish couldn't believe it. She'd never seen him this bad. Why had she told the other girls she was too sick to go job searching with them?

Mamm, who was so much shorter than he, tilted her head to look into his face. "I will not cook another breakfast when you have one on the table. There's nothing wrong with it."

"I don't want that one."

"Are you sure?"

"*Jah.*"

Mamm walked back to the table, picked up the plate of food and smashed it to the floor. Levi looked on in shock, and then *Mamm* walked out of the room.

"Cherish, I fear your *mudder* is having a breakdown. Call the bishop."

"If I call the bishop, I'll tell him what you've done."

When Levi looked like he was about to say something to her, she grabbed her last piece of toast and ran out the back door, ran out into the orchard and kept going.

She stopped when she was in the middle of the orchard and knew Levi wasn't coming after her. Never had she witnessed something so awful. The only thing she could think to do was talk to Florence. She made her way to the fence, climbed through, went up to the door and knocked on it wondering if it was too early to make a visit.

Carter opened the door scratching his head looking like he'd only just woken up.

"Carter, I'm so sorry to come. Am I too early?"

"What is it, Cherish?"

"Something weird and something horrible just happened."

He didn't look too worried. "Do you want me to get Florence for you?"

"Please."

He sat her in the living room in front of the fire and soon Florence came down wrapping her dressing gown ties around her waist.

"I'm so sorry, Florence, but it is important."

"What is it? Is everyone alright?"

"I think so, but I'm not sure. It was the weirdest thing."

"What happened?"

She repeated what happened over breakfast without embellishing it. "And then I just grabbed my toast and ran out. I didn't know what to do. Do you think *Mamm's* safe?"

"I think so. I don't think he would be violent."

"He dragged her across the room. That's violent if you ask me. Do you think you should go over there?"

Florence held onto her stomach and then stood up. Suddenly, she had her hand over her mouth and was running out the front door. Cherish followed her and watched her throwing up around the side of the house.

"What is it, Florence. Do you have food poisoning?"

Florence eventually straightened up. "I'm pregnant."

"You are?"

Florence smiled. "That's right."

"I'm going to be an aunt for the third time. This is so exciting, does Carter know?"

"Yes, we've known for a couple of weeks now, the baby is due in August."

"That's so exciting. I can't wait to tell *Mamm.*"

"We're not ready to tell anybody just yet. We're waiting a while. I didn't plan to tell you, but I didn't want you to worry that I might be sick or something."

"Would you like me to make you some hot tea?"

"Yes please."

"You okay now?"

"Yeah, I think so."

When they were both sitting in the kitchen, Florence sat down allowing Cherish to find her way around the kitchen. "Tell me more of what's been happening at home. I need the distraction from my morning sickness."

"Where's Carter?"

"He's probably gone back to bed. We had a bit of a late night. Everyone from his work came into town for the weekend."

"That's so good ... what were they like?" Cherish filled up the kettle.

"Really nice. They have tremendous respect for

Carter. I could tell that by the way they looked at him and the way they talked to him. Apart from regular meetings, each of them works from their own homes."

"That sounds great, at least I think so."

"I guess this place here's the central office."

"I'm so pleased. Everything is working out so well for you." When she flicked on the electric switch for the teakettle, she sat on the chair next to Florence.

"All of them were so welcoming to me."

"That's nice, but what should we do about, *Mamm?* Levi said she was having a breakdown, but she's not. He's just being horrible and impossible. I reckon she regrets marrying him, but it's too late, isn't it?"

"It is. They can't divorce, of course. They could separate, but since they haven't been married that long I'm sure the bishop will advise them to persevere."

"I don't want to be around while they're trying to work things out. This is just awful. And he made Matthew move out and stay over with Ada."

"I thought Matthew was staying with you?"

"He was, until last night. He sent him away." She

told him about Hope and Matthew being in the barn alone and Levi assuming the worst.

Florence shook her head.

"I wish she'd never married him. He's ruining all our lives. I might have coffee instead."

Florence rose to her feet. "I'll make it."

"Good. I'm tired of serving people. I do it all day at work and at home too. When can I tell everyone about the baby?"

"Not for another couple of months. Can you do that? Can you keep the news quiet?"

"Of course I can. Ooh, I hope Levi doesn't call the bishop and tell him *Mamm's* having a breakdown. She'll be so embarrassed. He told *me* to call him."

"I know. You said that. I think I would've walked out, too, at that point."

"You would've left *Mamm* there?"

"I'm sure she can look after herself. Maybe I should call Ada."

"Yes, Florence, do it. It's morning, so she should hear the phone ringing from her barn."

CHAPTER EIGHTEEN

hen Cherish left Florence's house to head home after two cups of coffee, she was pleased to see Ada's buggy there. She must've left to come over as soon as she hung up the phone from Florence. Florence hadn't said much to her, just that Levi had said that Wilma was having a breakdown after he'd dragged her across the kitchen. Hopefully Ada would be the voice of reason and tell Levi that he had to be nicer.

When Cherish got closer, she saw Ada getting out of the buggy. Cherish hurried over so she could get into Ada's ear before Levi did.

"What's going on?" Ada asked as soon as she saw Cherish.

"I was there when Florence called you. There's not much more to know about it than that."

"Levi called me just after I hung up from Florence. He said Wilma was having a hysterical moment. He said he thought it was change of life."

"Yeah, the change of life being that she changed her life by marrying him."

Ada pursed her lips.

Cherish couldn't hold back. "I think Levi is the one having the breakdown. You should've seen him. I don't blame *Mamm* for not making another breakfast for him. What a waste! There was nothing wrong with the first one. Many a time I've felt like upending the food on top of his head. He's impossible sometimes."

Ada looked down at the ground and shook her head. "This isn't good."

"I know."

"What I mean is that you're not helping."

Cherish had hoped that Ada was there to help, and now she was really worried. Was everyone going to be on Levi's side? Then her mother might have a breakdown for real. "Not helping Levi to be weird? I'm glad about that."

"I'm meant to be meeting the bishop here. He'll be here soon."

"He called the bishop too?"

"Yes, the bishop and his *fraa* are coming."

"Well, I don't think I'll be waiting around for that."

"That's best. Do you want to take my buggy and go somewhere for half an hour?"

"Nee, I will just go for a walk."

"Take my coat," Ada said pulling her own off. "You can't go around like that or you will catch your death of cold."

"Denke, Ada. I don't want to go back inside. Not until things calm down. This never happened between *Dat* and *Mamm.* They never had one argument, and they never disagreed about anything."

"Why talk about that? Your attitude is not helpful. You seem to be against Levi. Open your heart to Levi and to Bliss. It's not easy for them both to enter an established family."

She stared at Ada not knowing what to say. Bliss was okay, just barely sometimes, but she didn't want to open her heart to Levi. Why should she? He'd never been nice to her, and no one, not even her mother, deserved how he was treating her.

When Ada looked over at the house, she said, "I'll go in now."

"Okay. I'll disappear. *Denke* for the coat." Instead

of going for a walk, Cherish doubled back around and slipped in through the back door, so she could hear exactly what was going on. She stayed in the mud room until she heard the bishop and his wife arrive. Soon everyone was gathered in the living room and Cherish left her hiding spot and tiptoed through the kitchen so she could better hear what was going on.

Levi was the one who started talking first. "I'm not respected as the head of this household. Wilma's girls are always questioning my actions and they have no respect for me. Wilma is lazy and she's taught the girls to be the same."

"Tell him what you did about the breakfast this morning," Wilma said to him.

"It wasn't about the breakfast, Wilma. I was simply making you see that you should be making breakfast for me. Why is it up to the girls to make breakfast for me when I want my *fraa* to make it?"

The bishop said, "Does it matter who makes the breakfast, Levi?"

"It does to me."

Cherish got tired of standing when the conversation went back and forward, so she lowered herself to the floor to make herself comfortable. It was the best entertainment she'd had for a while. If only she could make them stop talking for a moment while she fixed herself a cup of coffee and grabbed some cookies.

A few minutes later, someone said something about making a pot of tea. Cherish scrambled to her feet and hid back in the mud room.

The bishop was getting nowhere and Cherish wondered what the outcome would be. Would they end up separating? Levi had such high standards but didn't notice his own daughter wasn't perfect. Instead of making a fuss about Wilma not making him breakfast, he should've been more worried about the fact that Bliss never helped with the breakfast, never helped with the baking, and only helped with the evening meal when she was asked.

When the bishop's wife left the kitchen with a tray of teas and coffees, Cherish left her hiding place and walked out of the house. It seemed no resolution existed for *Mamm* and Levi. It made Cherish all the more determined to make sure she married the right person for her. She was certain her mother had only married Levi because he'd been attentive to her.

Cherish found her dog, Caramel, asleep in the barn along with Joy's dog, Goldie. They had become an inseparable pair these days. Cherish sat down with them until she heard the front door open and close. She peeped out to see Ada was leaving.

She walked out of the barn and met her at her horse and buggy. "What happened?"

Ada looked up at her. "You girls are coming to stay with me for a while."

"We are?"

"The bishop has decided that Wilma and Levi need some time together to adjust."

"Oh. Is Bliss coming with us?"

"*Nee,* she's going to stay with Levi's *schweschder.*"

"What about Isaac and Joy?"

"I'm just off to see Christina now. They might be able to stay there. If not, they can stay with me, too."

"Okay. Shall I tell the other girls when they come home?"

"*Jah,* as soon as they come home, they can pack their bags. A week's worth of clothes. All of you, pack up and come to my place."

"*Denke,* Ada." She took off the coat and handed it back to her.

"We must open our minds and our hearts to people. Even people we don't like have problems and need our understanding."

Cherish nodded and then she felt a lick on her

hand. She looked down to see Goldie and Caramel had joined her. "What about the dogs?"

Ada frowned and looked down at the two dogs. "They'll stay here. It's only going to be a week or so."

There was no use arguing. "What about Timmy? Can I at least bring him? *Mamm* hates him and Levi never talks to him."

Ada sighed as she took hold of the reins. "I suppose one bird wouldn't do any harm."

"*Denke,* and he'll hardly take up any room."

When Ada left, Cherish didn't want to be around Levi, so she ran all the way to Fairfax's place. Then she successfully slipped past his parents' house without being seen and knocked on his door. He swung it open looking pleased. Then his face fell.

CHAPTER NINETEEN

*C*herish stared at Fairfax. "What is it? What's wrong?"

"Oh, I thought you were Hope."

"Hope?" She wasn't used to such rejection.

"Yes, come inside its cold out there." He walked over to the couch and she sat on an easy chair. "New furniture?"

"Yeah."

"I like them."

"Thanks."

"You're welcome."

He pushed aside two gamer's remote controls and sat down. "It's a bit difficult to tell you this, but I have spent time with Hope and then we had a disagreement."

145

"What about?"

"She thinks I was seeing you as well as her."

"You were seeing her ... as in dating? That sounds crazy. She never said anything to me. What's going on with the two of you?" She didn't believe her sister would be dating an *Englisher* without telling her.

"Nothing, now. I'll admit I like her. I was hoping she liked me too, and things were going great until my mother saw her and said, 'Hello, Cherish.'"

Cherish burst out laughing. "That's so funny. We don't look a thing alike."

She looked up at him and saw that he wasn't smiling or even laughing. "Oh, sorry. You're upset."

"I am. It's not funny. Hope doesn't believe nothing's going on with you and me." He narrowed his eyes at her. "How do you know my mother?"

"We had a nice talk once."

"Where did that occur?"

"At her house. I came here to see you and you weren't here and when I was leaving, I ran into her coming out of the house."

He shook his head.

"Don't worry, I'll sort this out with Hope. Trust me."

"You will?"

"Of course I will. I'm sure she likes you too, in case you were wondering."

"She does?"

"Mm-hmm."

"Did she say anything about me?"

"She didn't need to. I could just tell."

She had to say something to make him feel better.

"Anyway, enough about me and my problems. Why are you here?"

"I just had to get away from home for a moment. We're all going to stay at my mother's best friend's house for a while."

"Including Hope?"

"Yes, just us girls while my mother and new step-father work things out.

"It doesn't sound too good. Having problems, are they?"

Cherish nodded her head. "It's not good. Not at all."

"When are you going there?"

"As soon as the girls come home from wherever they are."

"Hope finishes work at two."

"What's the time now?

"It's just after two." He jumped to his feet. "You

should go now. It won't look good that you're at my house."

Cherish stood up.

"Please be sure to tell her that there's nothing going on between the two of us."

"Of course I will."

"Don't forget."

"I won't forget something like that." Cherish left the house and made her way home.

BY THE TIME Cherish got home, all the visitors had left the house. Levi was nowhere to be seen and none of her sisters was home yet.

"Is this what you want, *Mamm?*" whispered Cherish

"It's for the best,"

"Best for whom?"

"You'll understand when you're older."

"I don't know about that."

"Just make sure you make the right choice before you marry someone."

"Of course. Of course, I will."

"Don't be put off by Matthew. He is very nice."

"Matthew?" Cherish made a face. "I don't even like him. Not like that."

"Well you must find someone who does suit you."

"I will, *Mamm.* I've got plenty of time. Shouldn't you be concentrating on Hope?"

"Jah, you're right. Good girl."

"Don't worry." Cherish hugged her mother. "I'm sure things will sort themselves out."

"Yes, I'm sure they will. I'll need all of you girls to pray for me."

"We will."

They heard the sounds of a buggy coming toward the house. Cherish ran out and saw that Favor, Bliss and Joy had collected Hope. She told them all what was going on.

"I don't want to stay with Ada," said Favor.

"What are Isaac and I supposed to do?" asked Joy.

"Ada was asking Christina if you could stay there for a week."

"Ah, that's not so bad. I'm sure Christina and Mark won't mind."

She turned to Bliss who'd been very quiet. "Are you okay?"

"I'm upset. I thought our lives would be *wunderbaar* now. I finally had sisters."

Joy put her arm around her shoulders. "Things will work themselves out. Don't worry."

"You're going to your aunt's, Bliss."

Bliss rolled her eyes.

"That's what's been arranged. If you don't like it, talk to your father and he might be able to arrange something else."

"I don't see what the problem is," Bliss said.

Cherish stared at Bliss. "You can see they're not getting along."

"It's just that *Dat's* been in one of his moods. He's not always like that."

Cherish rolled her eyes.

Bliss gave Cherish a shove. "I saw that. It's true, he's not always like that."

"He should never be like that. Why should other people have to put up with his bad moods.?"

"Nobody is perfect. You're certainly not perfect."

"I never said I was," Cherish replied.

"Good." Bliss left the Baker girls and marched to the house.

"Can you believe her?" Cherish asked Favor.

"She's not so bad. She's just upset."

"You would say that because you're friends."

"We are all more than friends with her now," said Joy.

"I guess that's true. What's gonna become of us?" Favor whimpered.

"It's just a hiccup and then things will go back to normal."

Hope added, "And then we will just leave as soon as we are old enough."

"I like the way you're thinking. We could all move to my farm."

"Yes, I like the sound of that. But we can't live there with your caretaker. What will happen there?" asked Hope.

"Yes, that will be a bit sad for him. He'll have to move and go elsewhere."

"Oh, come on, Cherish. You'd be upset if you never saw him again. You talk about him all the time. It's always Malachi this, Malachi that. Everyone knows you're in love with him."

"I'm only talking about him because he's my caretaker. If he wasn't, I wouldn't give him two thoughts."

Favor patted the horse's neck. "I guess we're taking the horse and buggy to Ada's?"

"I guess so. And we'll use it while we're staying there."

"Okay."

"We have to get our things and go. We're having

dinner at Ada's."

"Poor *Mamm* staying here by herself," Favor said.

Joy said, "That's the point of it all. They need to be by themselves to work things out."

CHAPTER TWENTY

The next day at work, Hope was pleased about one thing. Favor was collecting her from work and driving her back to Ada's place. With not many guests at the bed and breakfast, Mrs. Jenkins had her polishing the silver until two and, with only fifteen minutes before going-home time, she was more than a little surprised when Fairfax walked into the room. She sat staring at him. This was unfair. She couldn't get away from him.

"What are you doing here?" she finally asked.

"I thought you might be pleased to see me."

"I'm working." She stared at him and didn't know what to say.

"Didn't Cherish talk to you?"

"About what?"

"She was going to talk with you."

"Are you saying you were talking to Cherish about me?"

"Yes."

Hope shook her head. "Please leave or I'll tell your aunt you're harassing me."

"Hope, I can explain. Cherish came to see me yesterday and I told her what happened with us and I found out that she met my mother."

"This is not something I want to hear."

He ran his hand through his hair. "Cherish was going to talk to you and sort this out. She promised me she would."

"Cherish hasn't told me anything about anything." She looked back at the silver and polished even harder, working the polish cloth into each of the crevices and curls of the patterned silver tray.

"I can't work out why she said she would and then she didn't."

"We had an upheaval last night. My sisters and I had to move to a friend's place."

"Not a fire?"

She shook her head. "Nee. It's a personal problem."

"Oh, one of those. Here's the truth." He pulled out a chair and sat down. "Cherish has been to see me a couple of times, but it's nothing more than friends. She sits down and just talks about nothing. She doesn't like me in that way, and I don't like her in that way. Anyway, she's far too young."

"Well, she's not that young."

"She is to me."

"Just forget about me, Fairfax. My life is complicated at the moment. And where you and I are concerned, there are too many differences."

"Hey, we've all got complicated lives."

"Not as complicated as mine."

She looked back at the tray, gave it a final polish and moved on to a teapot.

Jane walked in. "Fairfax, hi, I didn't know you were here."

"Yeah, hi." He jumped up and kissed his aunt on the cheek. "I just came to give your worker a ride home."

"You can go now if you like, Hope."

"No, it's okay thanks. I'll finish these last few."

"Suit yourself."

When Jane walked out of the room, Hope turned to Fairfax, and said, "One of my sisters is collecting me today."

"Oh, that's too bad. Where is this place you're staying?"

"Not too far."

He placed his hands on his hips. "Let me drive you tomorrow."

She looked up at his face and was tempted to say yes, but she knew it wasn't a good idea.

"It's madness, you riding a bike in the cold."

"No, it's not. A lot of people ride a bike in the winter, not only the summer."

"Let me take you, as a friend and nothing else. I won't say anything more, I'll not try to make you go out with me again. I'll just be a person taking you to where you're going."

She eyed him suspiciously.

"I mean it."

"No."

"Which sister is collecting you?"

"Cherish is at work doing a late shift if that's what you want to know."

"Hey, I already told you there's nothing going on there."

She shrugged her shoulders. "Thank you, but no thank you. I'll be fine. Forget about me."

"I'm at least pleased you won't freeze on your way home today."

"I won't." She kept her head down and kept scrubbing.

"I'm not giving up on you, Hope."

That caused her to scrub harder and then she realized he'd gone. She looked up at the clock and saw it was after four and not wanting to keep her sister waiting, she quickly packed up.

CHERISH YAWNED. She'd barely slept a wink last night sharing a bed with Favor who snored and flung her arms and legs about.

"Hey, Cherish," one of her co-workers said. "I'm taking that table."

She nodded to a man who'd just sat in Cherish's section. It was Fairfax. "No, I am. I know him."

"Yeah, well I'd like to get to know him."

Cherish grabbed her arm. "Too late, he already has a girlfriend." She hurried over to him leaving the other girl behind.

Fairfax had been scanning the menu and placed it down when she approached. "Cherish, hello."

"What are you doing here? You've never come here before. Have you come to see me?" Cherish stared down at his handsome face.

"Can I talk to you?"

"We're talking right now." She glanced over her shoulder. "You'll have to order something because my boss is watching. I'm on my last warning for talking to the customers too much." In a voice loud enough for her boss to hear, she recommended the carrot cake.

"Yeah fine, carrot cake, and a coffee."

In a low voice, she said, "I get off in half an hour if you can wait."

"Perfect."

She walked back past her boss and smiled. "I'm joining him when I clock off, is that okay?"

"Sure. What you do on your own time is no business of mine."

Half an hour later, she was sitting down with Fairfax. "Now, what's your problem?"

"Who said I have one?"

"I've never seen you look so down."

"You didn't say anything to Hope yet about why my mother knew your name."

"I was at your place and I met her." She threw her hands into the air. "It's not too difficult to figure out. Why all the fuss?"

"Yeah, well Hope thought the worst."

"It's not my problem."

"Cherish, one thing you don't understand is that I really like Hope."

She raised her eyebrows and picked up his cake

fork and stabbed some of his cake leftovers and then popped it into her mouth.

"Well, aren't you going to say anything?"

She pointed at her mouth. When she finished the mouthful, she said, "Morning …"

"It's actually afternoon."

"What I was saying was this morning she was speaking a lot with Matthew."

He leaned forward. "Should I be worried?"

"Yes."

He leaned back in his chair. "You'd better put this right." He pointed at her. "This is your fault."

"Hey, you were never gonna win. You're not Amish, he is. Everyone wants her to marry him. Except me, but only because I don't care who anyone marries."

"But what does *she* want? I know she likes me."

"It's ridiculous."

"What's ridiculous?"

"Going on feelings. I always feel I have a connection with everyone but obviously you can only marry one person, right?"

"I've never felt a connection with anybody else like I have with her."

"You'll find someone else."

He shook his head. "I don't want to."

Cherish giggled. "You'll fall in love again. I fall in love every other week."

"Everyone's not like you."

"The world would be a better place if everyone was."

One of the waitresses came over. "Can I get you a coffee, Cherish?"

"Yes please and another one for my friend. And, I might have something to eat." She looked at Fairfax. "You paying?"

He nodded.

"I'll have a cheese toastie and a chocolate cake with ice-cream."

"Sure. Anything else for you, sir?"

He shook his head. "Just the coffee thanks."

When the waitress left, he continued, "What I'm asking is that you need to set things right and tell Hope the truth. Tell her that we were never romantically involved." He shrugged his shoulders. "I can't believe she would even think that, but she does, so it's up to you to set her straight. She wouldn't listen to me. She'd think I was lying."

"Alright I'll tell her that … What do you want me to say again?"

"Why don't we start off with the truth?"

"Ah yes, the truth … Truth is a funny thing." She

set the cake fork down on the table and spun it around in a circle. "There's your truth, my truth, and then there's the truth in the middle." She smiled at him. "Whoever has the prongs of the fork pointing at them is a liar."

The waitress set the two coffees down in front of them.

When she left, Fairfax grabbed the cake fork. "What are you talking about, Cherish?"

"That's just something that my father used to say. He was a very wise man. Nothing like Levi. Oh, and he didn't do that thing with the fork. I just made that up." She giggled at herself.

"Can we keep on topic? The topic is, you telling Hope that nothing has ever happened between us and nothing ever will. And tell her how you came to meet my mother. Can you just do that?" He placed the fork down on the other side of the table out of her reach.

She saw how frustrated he was and she took a sip of cappuccino. "You really do like her, don't you?"

"How many different ways do you have to be told? Of course I like her."

"Okay, I'll tell her, but it's probably too late. She's probably accepted Matthew's proposal of marriage."

"She'll just have to un-accept it."

"For what? For you?"

"Yes, for me. Tell me, what do I have to do to win her heart?"

"Just be decent, I guess."

"I am. But she must see that. It was fine until the whole debacle over my mother calling her Cherish. It was the last straw for her. The first straw and the last."

"I will tell her as soon as I see her next."

"When will that be?"

"This afternoon or tonight. As soon as I can, I will. Okay?"

"Thank you, Cherish."

Cherish rolled her eyes. The whole thing was boring. Why did Hope have to be so dramatic? And why couldn't Fairfax be captivated with her instead of Hope? Not that she was captivated by him, but still ...

CHAPTER TWENTY-ONE

When Cherish finished work she hurried out to Joy's waiting buggy with a take-out hot chocolate in each hand. It was nice to see Joy's smiling face. Not one of them had smiled since their mother got married, she was sure of that.

"I got you a hot chocolate."

"Denke. That'll help warm me up."

"Have you heard anything from them?" Cherish asked as she climbed into the buggy.

"No I haven't. I've been helping Christina all day. I'll come in and talk to Ada when I get there."

"Good thinking. She'll be up on what's going on."

Joy warmed her hands around the cup then opened the lid and had a sip. "What does Ada think about what's happened with *Mamm* and Levi? Has she mentioned anything?"

"*Nee,* she's not really saying anything. She'd have her opinion but she's not going to share it with us."

"Hold this for me for a minute." Joy passed her cup to Cherish and then clicked the horse forward.

"I wonder how long we'll be staying with Ada."

"I don't know. It depends on what's going on at home."

Cherish let out a loud sigh. "I didn't get any sleep last night, sharing a small bed with Favor."

"When does Matthew go home?"

"He leaves later today sometime."

"Then you can have his bed."

"I hope so. He's in love with Hope. He'll be sad to leave. It seems everybody is in love with her and no one's in love with me."

Joy laughed. "You'll have plenty of people in love with you soon. There's plenty of time."

"Yeah, only people I don't like."

Once they were on a straight road, Joy put her hand out for the hot chocolate. "Don't talk like that. I'm positive you'll have someone who likes you very soon. I've never known you to be lacking for male attention anyway."

"Yeah, well things have changed a bit lately. Why does Levi have to be so horrible?"

Joy took a mouthful. "You shouldn't say that, Cherish."

Cherish settled into the seat and drank her hot chocolate, while thinking about every horrible thing Levi had ever done or said. When they reached Ada's house, they were surprised to see their mother's buggy.

"What's *Mamm* doing here?" Cherish stared at the buggy. Had she given up on trying to sort things out with Levi? If so, she couldn't blame her. Maybe now things would go back to normal.

"I don't know, let's go and see."

After Joy secured the buggy, the two sisters walked into the kitchen. *Mamm* and Ada, were sitting with Favor, Hope and Isaac.

"What are you doing here, *Mamm?*"

Ada spoke for her. "She's come to take you girls home."

Cherish gasped. She'd been right.

"Home?" Joy asked. "Will Isaac and I go back too?"

"Jah, if you want to."

"Good."

"What about Levi?" asked Cherish.

There was a strained silence. Even Ada had nothing to say. Eventually, *Mamm* spoke. "I'll tell you girls what's happening on the way home. Gather your things."

That was more than Cherish could stand; she hated not knowing things.

Before the girls left, they were saying goodbye to Matthew, who was leaving very soon to go home.

He surprised everyone by asking Hope if he could talk to her in private.

HOPE WAS a little embarrassed when she followed Matthew away from the others to talk. When he got to the barn, he turned around to face her. "Hope, would you write to me?"

"*Jah*, I will."

"You've always been special to me."

She looked down at her lace-up shoes, absently noting that the lacing patterns didn't match one another, not knowing what to say. There were many reasons he would make a good match for her, but how could she commit to him when she still had feelings for Fairfax? Even though Fairfax wasn't a very trustworthy kind of person she couldn't shake the feelings she had for him. She looked back up at

Matthew. "I will write to you, but I can't make any promises. Don't stop thinking about other girls just for me, if you know what I mean."

"I would do that if you asked me."

She shook her head. "Let's just see what happens. We'll write to one another and then we will meet again sometime."

"Sometime soon?"

She looked over her shoulder at everybody watching them. "Maybe. I'd give you a goodbye hug but everyone's watching."

He chuckled. "I understand. I'd give you one back, but ... well, everyone's watching."

They exchanged smiles and then walked back to Wilma, Ada and the girls. Then when everyone hugged Matthew goodbye, Hope got to give him a quick hug too. The car was coming soon to take him to the train station.

Joy and Isaac went back to Christina's place, while Wilma took her other daughters home.

Cherish didn't want to be the one to ask what was going on with Levi, and since the other girls were quiet, they must've been thinking the same way.

. . .

WHEN MAMM STOPPED the buggy in front of the barn, she finally spoke. "Levi isn't here tonight. He's at his old home with Bliss." The girls waited for her to say more and Cherish couldn't resist being the first to ask for more. "Go on. Does that mean …"

"LEVI and I have worked things out. I'm going away for a while. It's best we have time apart. Don't tell anyone we're having problems. All will be okay. I'm staying with a friend in Ohio, Dulcie."

"Dulcie's dochder is one of my pen pals. Can I come?" Favor asked.

"I thought you'd stay here, *Mamm,* if Levi's gone home," said Cherish.

Mamm shook her head. "I've got a lot of thinking and praying to do."

"Can't you do that here?" asked Hope.

"Nee, I can't."

"Take me with you, *Mamm?"* Favor asked once more.

"Nee."

"Well, can I have one of my other pen pals come stay while you're gone?"

"Stop bothering *Mamm.* It's not a good idea to

have visitors at this time." Hope gave a firm nod to Favor who was in the backseat of the buggy.

"How long will you be and who's going to keep things going here?" asked Favor. "And will Joy and Isaac come back?"

"I expect so. I might be gone for a while. If I don't go to Dulcie's I might go to stay with Mercy for when her baby comes. That way I'll be close to Honor too. I'm waiting on a call back from them. Also Joy and Isaac can come back any time they choose. They didn't have to leave."

"What about the orchard? What's happening there?" asked Hope.

Favor suggested, "Maybe we should get a manager in to look after the orchard."

"Florence could do it," Cherish said. "She's honestly the perfect person for the job."

"Florence no longer has anything to do with this family. There are other people who can do the same thing. Levi was right about one thing; you girls shouldn't have been so lazy and then one of you could've taken over and stepped into Florence's shoes when she left." *Mamm* got out of the buggy. "Hope, you and Favor can tend to the horse."

"You've never said anything like that before to us," Hope said. "About being lazy."

"Well, it's not good, is it, if we have to employ someone? It's money leaving the household."

"Maybe if the three of us all work together we could figure it all out between us," Favor said, as she stepped out of the buggy.

"Three girls doing the job of one?" *Mamm* shook her head. "Levi would have a lot to say about that."

"*Jah,* and we all know he has a lot to say about everything." Cherish jumped when Hope glared at her, and she said, "Sorry, *Mamm.*"

Their mother sighed. "He's part of the family and you girls need to treat him that way. We just have to hope that we have a good harvest this year. You girls are the cause of most of the arguments between Levi and me."

"We'll try to do …" Favor's voice trailed off as their mother stomped to the house. "She's not listening to me. No one ever listens to me."

"You've got to be bolder," Cherish told her. "You're too shy."

"It's just the way I am."

"I'll go talk to *Mamm,* make sure she's okay." Cherish hurried to the house in case the girls asked her to help unhitch the buggy. Then she remembered she'd left Timmy in the buggy. She turned on her heel.

"You helping now?" Hope asked.

"Nee. Mamm only said for you both to do it. I've had a hard day at work."

"Yeah, well, don't you think I've had a harder day? I have to clean and all you do is serve coffee and smile at people and flirt to get large tips."

Cherish reached in and pulled out Timmy's cage. "We share the tips and I don't flirt with people."

"Do so," added Favor.

"I'm just naturally friendly. My boss even mentioned the way I talk to people."

"Jah, probably told you to zip it," Hope said with a grin.

Favor laughed and then so did Hope, so Cherish just walked away from them. When she walked inside, she was greeted by her dog and Joy's dog. "Hello, guys. It's good to be home. Has Wilma been looking after you?" she asked as she carried the bird through to the kitchen.

"It's *Mamm* to you," her mother said.

"Jah, sure, *Mamm.* Did you look after Caramel and Goldie?" She hung the birdcage on its stand and turned around to look at her mother who was pulling vegetables out of the cupboard.

"They're still alive, aren't they?"

Cherish looked down at them. *"Jah."*

"Help me with these vegetables."

"Sure." She sat down with a knife and cutting board. "Before the others come in, tell me what's going on with you and Levi."

"There's nothing to tell that I haven't already said. We've talked everything through, and things will be fine."

"I'm glad." Cherish wasn't convinced. How could things go from bad to not bad in the space of one day? Her mother wasn't telling her everything.

CHAPTER TWENTY-TWO

*D*uring the after-dinner washing up, Cherish remembered what she had promised Fairfax regarding Hope. Now, with her washing and Hope drying, she had a perfect opportunity.

"Hope, when Fairfax's mother thought I was you that's because she hadn't met you and she must've thought that we look similar."

Hope stopped drying the plate in her hands. "But how do you know her?"

"I went there looking for him one day."

"For what?"

"I can't remember now. I think I was just bored or something." Cherish had been tempted to lie and say she was meeting him to ask him to buy the horse, but that would mean another lie she'd have to cover up later on.

"That explains it."

"What else did you think?"

"Wait a minute, you would only know she called me Cherish if Fairfax has told you. So, you have been in contact with him?"

This was getting more complicated by the moment. She remembered that someone once said that if you were going to lie about something you had to have a good memory. Her memory wasn't so good, so she decided to tell the truth. "He came to the coffee shop today because he was dreadfully upset. He really likes you. And he doesn't want you to marry Matthew."

"I'm not marrying Matthew. Where did you get that from?"

"That's where I saw things going."

"You didn't tell Fairfax that, did you?"

"*Nee. Jah.* I can't remember."

Hope shook her head. "It's not going to happen. We've only been talking because I feel bad about Levi sending him away."

"I don't really care who you marry or don't marry. I'm only saying that because he was so upset. He doesn't like me and never has."

"*Denke* for telling me. I was a bit worried."

"Well, do you like him as much as he seems to like you?"

She looked around to see if they could be overheard. When she saw that there was no one else in the kitchen, she continued, "Kind of, but I don't know if there's any point pursuing anything, if you know what I mean."

"Because he's an *Englisher?*"

Hope nodded and continued drying the dishes. "Matthew seems nice and very kind. He didn't deserve to be treated the way Levi treated him. It was embarrassing."

"What are you two girls doing? I don't think you should be talking about Matthew. He was sent away from the house for a reason."

They both swung around to see their mother had just walked in. It seemed she'd heard every word.

"Yeah, he was sent away from here for no *good* reason," Cherish said.

"Hold your tongue, girl. When you're finished, come out to the living room with the rest of us. I have an announcement to make."

"What is it?" asked Cherish.

"You'll find out with the rest of them." With that, *Mamm* left the kitchen.

Cherish turned back to the saucepan she'd been scrubbing. "What do you think it would be?" she asked Hope.

"I think they're going to separate for good."

"Nee. They'd never do that."

"Things turned bad pretty quick."

"Jah, but *Mamm* said everything was going to be okay with the two of them." Cherish looked back at the saucepan, figured it was cleaned well enough, rinsed the soap from it quickly and passed it to Hope. She then pulled the plug out to drain the warm sudsy water, giving the sink a quick rinse before she shook her hands dry.

Hope wiped the pan and put it away in the cupboard, then she stood next to Cherish who hadn't moved from the sink. Their eyes met in a silent exchange. They were both worried about what their mother had to say. Somehow, they both knew it would change all of their lives.

Placing her arm gently around Cherish's shoulders, Hope said, "Come on let's get this over with."

CHAPTER TWENTY-THREE

*L*ater that night when they were gathered in the living room, *Mamm* said, "I was going to tell you over dinner, but I didn't. I'm not going to Dulcie's now. I had a call from Mercy and I've been invited to stay with her and Stephen for when she has the *boppli*."

"How long will you be gone?" Hope asked.

"I'm thinking of leaving soon."

"Are we going with you?" Favor asked.

"*Nee*. You'll stay here and continue to look for work."

"I already have a job," said Cherish.

"Then you can continue to look for a full-time job just as Levi told you to."

Hope left where she was sitting and squashed herself in between Favor and their mother. "When will you be back?"

"When Mercy and Honor no longer need me."

Cherish knew it would be impossible with *Mamm* gone. How would they put up with Levi? "Is Levi coming back here while you're gone?"

"*Jah,* this is his home. Everything will go back to normal. Joy and Isaac will come back to live here, too, just like before."

"Do you have to go see them?" Cherish whined.

"I do. My first two *dochders* are having their first *bopplis.* I want to be there."

"When's Levi coming back?" asked Hope.

"He and Bliss will be here tomorrow. We'll have a nice family dinner tomorrow and Joy and Isaac will eat with us too. Everyone leaving was a temporary thing." Wilma covered her mouth and yawned, and then stared into the distance for a moment. "I might have an early night. Everything that's happened over the past couple of days has worn me out."

"Good idea, *Mamm.* I'll bring you up a hot cup of tea," Hope said.

When *Mamm* headed upstairs the girls went into the kitchen. Anxiety began to churn at Cherish's stomach.

"This is not good," whispered Hope to Cherish and Favor, as she fired up the stove and set the filled teakettle on it.

Favor sighed. "I know, but there's nothing we can do about it. We'll have to make the best of it. I wish *Mamm* had never married Levi."

Hope nodded. "Me too, but we can't turn back time."

"I wish we could."

Favor said, "I heard Bliss call *Mamm, 'Mamm'* the other day. It was weird."

The Baker girls looked at one another. "That would've been weird," Hope said.

"It was."

"*Mamm's* getting away, escaping. What if she never comes back?" Cherish said.

Hope dug Cherish in the ribs. "Don't even say it."

"She'll come back. She has to." Favor started chewing on her fingernails.

"Why would she return? She doesn't like me, Joy's married, and she doesn't want to be married to Levi anymore."

"There's me and Hope," Favor said. "She'd have to come back for us."

"It'd be weird hearing Bliss call her *Mamm*. I mean, she's *not* her *mudder*."

"Cherish, that's the least of everyone's problems," Hope told her. "We should all talk about this later when *Mamm's* asleep. I wouldn't want her to overhear us."

"What are you going to do about Fairfax?" asked Cherish.

"Nothing."

"Fairfax?" asked Favor looking confused.

"*Jah*, he's in love with Hope," Cherish whispered. "Go see him, Hope. He'll think I haven't said anything and then he'll keep coming back to the café."

"I'm still not convinced." Hope shook her head.

"What? I'm not lying."

"Yeah? You have lied in the past."

Cherish knew she had a point. She could've been lying but she wasn't. "I'm not lying now."

"If he was in love with me, I'd go see him." Favor put her hand over her mouth and giggled.

Hope said to Cherish, "Okay, I'll trust you because I do believe you. But I'm still not going out of my way to see him. If I happen to bump into him somewhere, then well and good."

"He's not Amish," Favor said as though it had suddenly dawned on her.

Cherish poked Favor in her ribs causing her to jump. "She knows that."

Favor shrugged her shoulders. "I was just saying it. No need to hurt me."

CHAPTER TWENTY-FOUR

*T*he next morning, Hope didn't want to ask anyone to take her to work. Besides, if Levi found out she wasn't riding the bike, it might create even more problems within the family.

To help shield herself from the cold, she'd worn two pairs of extra thick stockings and two layers of undergarments, as well as her thick black coat.

Just when she was getting into the rhythm of things and thinking about what was to become of her family, a vehicle passed her. She soon saw it was Fairfax's pickup truck. He stopped the truck in front of her, opened his door and walked back.

"Hi, Hope."

She stopped her bike and got off. "Hello."

"Did Cherish sort things out with you?"

Secretly she was pleased he'd gone to so much bother. "She did."

"Great, so you understand?"

"It's fine. It's all fine. You really don't need to worry." She got on her bike again.

"Like a ride?"

The offer certainly was tempting. Levi would never find out and besides, she'd have a chance to tell Fairfax that nothing could come of anything. They couldn't have a relationship. "Sure." She got off the bike and saw him grinning.

He picked up the bike with one swift motion and placed it carefully onto the bed of his truck.

She slid into the passenger seat wondering where to begin. When he got back onto the road, she said, "Thank you for getting me the job. That was good of you."

He glanced over at her. "Glad I could be of service."

"Yes, well you were and I'm grateful, but we can't be friends."

"Good, because I don't want to be friends."

Immediately she was disappointed. "You don't?"

"I want to be much more than friends."

Secretly, she was pleased.

"Do I need to become Amish or something?"

184

She looked at him out of the corner of her eye. Young men like him never joined their community. Even Carter hadn't, even though he loved Florence. "Well, it's not as simple as that."

"Life is what you make it. You can do anything or achieve anything you want. If you can see it, you can believe it. No, wait a minute. I think that last one is the other way around."

She laughed. "It sounded good anyway."

Then they arrived at her work. He stopped the truck and she said, "Could you get the bike out for me?"

"No need."

"Why? I can't walk home."

He smiled at her. "I'll drive you home."

She opened her door halfway and felt the cold air. It was too tempting an offer to refuse. "Okay. Thank you."

He grinned. "I'll be here at two sharp. Have a great day." He jumped out, ran around and held the door open for her.

CHAPTER TWENTY-FIVE

When Florence heard a buggy coming up her driveway, she secretly imagined it being Wilma having second thoughts about getting to know her son. That was her hope every time she heard a buggy. How wonderful it would be if they could all get along.

She hurried to the window and looked out to see it was Christina. All that morning she had been feeling queasy with morning sickness. Carter had gone out to get her some medicine from the pharmacy and she was still in her dressing gown. She opened the door. Christina had something in her hands wrapped in a tea towel. Florence guessed it was a pie.

Christina stepped onto the porch and looked Florence up and down. "Did I wake you up?"

"No, I was awake."

"Late night?"

"No." The last thing she wanted to do was tell Christina she was pregnant. Christina and Mark had been trying to have a baby for years with no success.

"I brought a peach pie," Christina extended the pie to her.

The thought of the sweet fruit in the golden flakey pie crust turned Florence's stomach and she ran past Christina, flew down the steps and threw up in the garden beds at the front of the house.

Christina placed the red and white tea towel wrapped pie on the floor of the porch and ran to her. "Florence! Are you alright?"

Florence stared up wiping her mouth with the back of her hand. "No. Carter has gone to the pharmacy for me. I have some kind of a stomach bug, I think."

Christina eyed her suspiciously. "You're not pregnant, are you?"

She slowly nodded hoping Christina wouldn't cry hysterically. She wouldn't be able to cope with it.

"That is wonderful news."

Florence was relieved. "Thank you. We haven't told anybody yet. Only Cherish knows."

"Cherish?"

"She guessed."

"If she knows, everybody must know by now."

"If any of the others knew they'd be knocking on the door. I think she's actually kept it to herself."

"That is surprising. Are you alright to come back into the house where it's warm?"

"I think so." She rose to her feet and Christina helped her back into the living room. Christina then went back outside to fetch the pie. She placed it in the kitchen before she joined Florence on the couch.

"This is exciting news. And when were you go to tell me?"

"I was a little hesitant. You've told me before how you hate it when people get pregnant or you hear of people who are pregnant."

"It is a little frustrating, but we're family, so that's different. I get to cuddle the baby, so that makes some difference."

Florence felt sorry for her sister-in-law. Although she was smiling, her eyes told the truth of her secret pain. "You'll certainly get to cuddle the baby." Florence rubbed her slightly swollen belly.

"How far along are you?"

"Not far. The baby is due in early August."

"You've got a long way to go. Your two sisters have beat you to it."

Florence chuckled. "That doesn't bother me in the slightest. I just feel so blessed that I have such a good husband and we're about to have a baby. And I'm happy. Three things I never thought would happen to me."

"You deserve it, Florence."

"Thank you, it's nice to hear someone say that."

"So, Wilma still hasn't visited you?"

"A couple of times, but not for social reasons. She comes if she's got something to say and that's not very often."

"Can I tell Mark about the baby?"

"Of course you can. And then I will have to call Earl and tell him too. Can't have Mark knowing without Earl knowing."

"I do envy you Florence, not in a bad way, but in a good-natured way. I would love it to happen for me. I just don't know why it isn't. I'm believing for it as hard as I can."

"Sometimes things like that are a mystery to me. You can pray really hard for things and sit by and watch other people get what you want. It hardly seems fair, there seems no rhyme or reason."

"Yeah, everyone says God has a plan, so is His plan to keep me childless forever? What do I have to do ... what do I have to learn ... what is it He wants to teach me?"

"I don't know. Maybe nothing." She felt sorry for her always being in such torment. "Have you thought about adopting?"

"We have. We've talked about adopting and we've talked about fostering."

"That sounds wonderful. Either one of those sounds like a good idea."

"Do you think so?"

"I do."

"Mark's not so keen. We both go back and forth; when I'm not keen, he is." She sighed.

"Maybe you're both sensing each other's apprehension or indecision. If you make up your mind that's what you want and then tell him, I'm sure he'll be happy with whatever you decide."

"Do you think so?"

"I do. And you'd both make wonderful parents."

A smile met Christina's lips. "Do you think so?"

"Yes, I do."

When they heard a car, Christina said, "That must be Carter now. I hope he found you something to take."

"Me too. I just get it in the morning and then it passes, but while it's here it's dreadful."

"I should leave."

"You can stay."

"Nee. It was only a quick visit."

"Thank you for stopping by, and thank you for that …" She put her hand over her mouth. She couldn't even say the word. "The thing you left in the kitchen."

"You're welcome." Christina giggled. "I'll come again in a few days to see how you are. If you need anything let me know. I can start sewing for your baby."

"That would be lovely. I would appreciate that, Christina. Your sewing is beautiful."

"Did you ever get your …?" She swiped a hand through the air. "It doesn't matter we can talk about that later." She stood and kissed Florence on the top of her head. "Keep well."

"I'll try."

"Don't get up."

Florence sat quietly next to Spot who was sleeping on the couch beside her. Once Christina was outside, she heard Carter and Christina talking.

Then Carter walked through the door smiling.

"Did you get something?" she asked.

"B6."

"What's that?"

"It's a vitamin."

"No, I need more than that."

He crouched down in front of her. "We've already got everything they suggested. As well as all the herbs, teas and potions anyone ever thought of or invented."

"Okay, I'll try it."

He handed her the bottle. "I'll get you some water."

CHAPTER TWENTY-SIX

The family dinner the Baker girls were dreading came that very night. Bliss and Levi had moved back in while Hope was at work, and so had Joy and Isaac. The house was full once more.

Levi had piled his plate high with food, as though he hadn't eaten when he was away. "I think that you girls will have to slip into Wilma's shoes while she's gone, and help out more around here."

"As well as still looking for jobs?" Cherish asked.

"That's right. Many women have full-time jobs and run a household by themselves."

Joy cleared her throat. "Well, I was wondering … I had this idea that Isaac and I could have our own space if we put a caravan here on the land somewhere."

Levi's face contorted. "A caravan?" He looked over at Wilma. "Did you hear that?"

"This is the first I'm hearing about it."

"We wanted to ask you both together to see what you think," Isaac said. "I found a caravan we can lease and they can deliver it here. I can take out a year's lease and then by that time we would've saved enough for a place of our own."

Levi moved uncomfortably in his chair obviously not liking the idea.

Cherish knew Levi was thinking about the money he'd lose if they did that.

"What do you think about the idea?" Joy asked.

Levi tilted his head. "I don't know what I think about the idea. I'll have to think it over."

"*Jah,* we'll pray on it."

Levi looked directly at Isaac. "We will let you know tomorrow morning."

"If the answer is no, we could find someone else's land to put the caravan on," Joy said.

Mamm shook her head. "It makes little sense. Why live in a tiny little caravan when you can live in a big house with a fireplace? You'll freeze to death in a caravan."

"We want to be alone, *Mamm.*"

"We give you privacy. You've got a whole room to yourselves. And it's only for one year."

"That's true," Isaac said, "but we'd save more this way."

Levi raised his hand in a motion to silence everyone. "As I said, I'll give you my answer in the morning."

Mamm shook her head once more. "It's going to look untidy. People will wonder why we have a caravan in the yard. It'll be odd you living there when there's a perfectly good *haus* you can stay in."

"Wilma, that's enough talk about it," Levi growled.

Cherish stared at him. He hadn't changed at all. Their father never would've spoken to their mother like that. "When are you leaving, *Mamm?*" Cherish asked, mostly to change the direction of the conversation.

"In the next couple of days. We have to make the travel arrangements first."

Cherish was surprised that Levi was allowing her to leave. But at the same time, she knew her mother needed a break.

CHAPTER TWENTY-SEVEN

When the day came for their mother to leave, Cherish was much more upset than she thought she would be. They were all there to see her off except Hope and Isaac who'd both left for work.

Cherish hugged her mother tightly at the door while they waited for the car to arrive. "Do you really have to go?"

"I told your sisters I would."

"Who cares about them?"

"I do. If you were having your first *boppli* wouldn't you want me to be there for you?"

"I wouldn't have left here. They're the ones who have left, so they should suffer the consequences of their actions." She looked around for Levi. "Isn't that right, Levi?"

"What's that?"

"I said the girls left, so *Mamm* shouldn't have to go running after them."

He laughed. It was very rare to see him laugh and that made Cherish a bit happier.

"Your *mudder* has her mind made up. And when she has her mind made up there's a little anyone can do about anything."

"It's my turn now." Favor pushed Cherish aside to hug her mother.

"If I knew I would have this much attention going away I'd go away more often." Wilma laughed.

"We will miss you, *Mamm,*" said Joy.

"I'm not dying, I'll be back soon."

Favor asked, "How soon after the babies are born will you come back?"

"I don't really know, that depends how things go. If it all goes well, I might be back a couple of months after."

"A couple of months?" Cherish screeched.

"That's right. Don't forget there'll be two *bopplis* and I have to divide myself between the two households."

The place wouldn't be the same without her.

There would only be the three of them in the house now with Joy and Isaac living in the caravan. Four girls in the house including Bliss.

"Here's the car now," said Levi squinting down to the end of the driveway.

Bliss hugged Wilma and then joined the girls who were huddled together.

Cherish turned away so she wouldn't see her mother and her stepfather embracing. They seemed to be getting on better. Maybe absence would make their hearts grow fonder. Levi might miss her, and treat her nicely when she came back ... and time away would cause her mother to forget what he'd done and how he'd spoken to her.

Levi then put the luggage in the trunk and paid the driver.

They watched the car leave and *Mamm* waved until she was out of sight. Just as the car was going around the corner out of sight, the truck pulling the caravan appeared.

"Joy, look, your caravan's here."

Joy jumped up and down with excitement and then both dogs jumped up at her.

Cherish watched for a while from the porch and then moved to the living room where it was warmer. Levi took over, directing the truck to back up and get the caravan in the exact right spot behind the barn. *Mamm* had wanted it out of sight, so no one could see it from the road. Isaac and Joy didn't care where it went.

An hour later, the caravan was all set up and the girls helped move Isaac and Joy's things in. When Cherish stepped up into the caravan, she was surprised to see how much room there was. There was a built-in kitchen, operated by gas, with a built-in table with bench seats, and at the end there was a double bed as well as a small bathroom. "It's got everything here that you could want." Cherish turned around to look at Joy.

"I know, it's perfect. Just what I wanted."

"You might never move out," said Favor.

"It's cold," complained Bliss.

"By tonight, it'll be toasty warm in here. It's got gas and Isaac is bringing a heater home with him."

Bliss raised her eyebrows. "Is he? Must be made of money."

"If we were made of money, we'd have our own home. It won't be long. A year, Isaac said, and we'll be in our own home. I'm going to look for a job and that will help us save."

"There are so many of us looking for jobs. Why

don't you wait until all of us get our jobs before you start looking?" Bliss suggested.

"I'll think about that, Bliss."

Cherish smiled. Maybe she could learn a thing or two from Joy.

"Come on, we've got more to collect from the *haus*." Joy jumped out of the caravan and the other girls followed.

CHAPTER TWENTY-EIGHT

A week later, Bliss and Levi were visiting his sister for the day and Cherish made a suggestion. She looked around at Joy and Favor, who still hadn't found jobs. "Why don't we visit Florence? We haven't seen her in ages, and she doesn't know that *Mamm's* gone away."

"*Jah,* we've got so much to tell her," said Favor.

Cherish shut the dogs in the house so they wouldn't follow them, and they all walked through the orchard. "I'll race you to the fence." Cherish started running before she'd finished talking, but even so, Favor managed to beat her to the fence.

"I'm first." Then Favor tried to get through the wires and snagged the bottom of her dress.

"Careful." Joy helped her unhook the dress from the barbed wire.

ONCE THEY WERE all through the fence, they made their way to the house. "The car's gone. I hope she's home."

"Yeah, well, she might be. I've got a feeling she'll be home since it's still morning."

Favor stared at Cherish. "Why do you say that?"

"No reason in particular."

Joy said, "What are you up to, Cherish? Do you know something we don't know?"

"*Jah,* I know a lot more than the both of you put together." Cherish giggled. "Race everyone to the house." She ran ahead of them so she wouldn't have to answer any more questions.

Florence answered the door, still in her dressing gown and slippers.

"How are you, Florence?" Joy asked.

"I'm fine. Come inside. It's nice to see you. Is everything okay?"

"It is. We've got a lot to tell you. I'll put the kettle on."

Once they all had hot tea, they sat in the living room. "What's going on?" Florence asked.

Cherish told her everything that had happened, and that *Mamm* had gone to be with Mercy and Honor for the arrivals of their babies.

"*Jah,* and Isaac and I got the caravan. Thanks for that idea. Levi allowed me to have it at the house, but *Mamm* insisted it had to be out of sight, behind the barn."

"Oh, that's good. I'm glad they didn't say no."

"It was your idea, Florence?" asked Favor.

"*Jah,* it was her idea but don't go telling anyone," Joy said.

"I won't."

"Also, another thing that's happened is that Joy's not so high and mighty anymore."

Joy narrowed her eyes at Cherish. "What do you mean?"

"I've noticed a change in you since Levi moved in. You were always the good one and you'd never speak out against anyone."

"*Jah,* she's right, Joy. I noticed that too, but I didn't realize it until Cherish said so. You always used to quote Scriptures and now you don't so much anymore."

"I still think them. I don't say them because everyone got annoyed with me."

Florence sipped her tea, battling nausea. Nothing

much had changed with the girls. They were still the same. "Where's Hope?"

"She's got a job at a bed and breakfast," Joy said.

"She's in love with Fairfax."

"Nee, he's in love with her," Cherish corrected Favor.

Favor bounded to her feet with her hands clenched into fists. "Why do you treat me like an idiot? I'm not."

"I'm just saying you're wrong. I didn't call you an idiot."

"Yeah, you just thought it."

"Sit down," Joy told her.

"Nee. They're all mean to me, Florence."

Florence couldn't take it anymore. She knew she was going to be sick. She dropped her hot tea on the floor and ran outside hoping to make it in time.

She sank to her knees and threw up, not once but twice. Then she sat on the cold ground.

Cherish ran out with a handful of tissues, and Florence wiped her mouth. The other two just stared at her in disbelief. After a moment, she stretched out her arms to Cherish for help getting to her feet.

"What's wrong?" Favor asked.

Joy stepped forward. "Ooh, Florence. Are you pregnant?"

She nodded. "I am."

The girls jumped up and down excitedly, congratulating her.

All Florence could do was hold her head, feeling a little worse for wear.

"Should we go and leave you to rest?" asked Cherish.

"No. Please stay a bit."

They all went back inside, and Favor went to make her another cup of tea, while Joy cleaned up the spilled tea.

"Where's Spot?" asked Cherish.

"He's with Carter, having his vaccinations at the vet."

When Joy sat back down, she said, "When is the baby due?"

"Early August."

"Can we tell *Mamm?*" asked Favor as she passed Florence the fresh cup of tea.

"I guess so. It can't hurt."

"She'll be thrilled," said Joy.

Florence wasn't so certain about that.

"*Jah,* this'll be *Mamm's* step-grandchild and her biological one too. Double reasons to be pleased."

"Tell me what else is happening."

"I'm thinking about another visit to the farm," Cherish said.

"*Nee,* Cherish, you've just come back. There's no reason for you to keep going back there so much. I need one of my pen pals to visit before anyone does anything else."

"I've got a better idea. Why don't you go visit one of your pen pals and then we can all have some peace?"

Favor's mouth dropped open at Cherish's words. "Why be so mean?"

"Oh, that's right, because no one's invited you to visit, have they?"

Florence looked at Favor to see her looking crushed. "I'm sure they have and if they haven't that would only be because they would think Favor wouldn't be permitted to visit them."

Favor smiled.

When Cherish had just opened her mouth to speak again, Joy bounded to her feet. "We should go now, and leave Florence to rest."

"I haven't finished my tea yet," said Cherish.

"It doesn't matter. Florence can't rest with all this arguing going on."

"I wasn't arguing," Favor said.

"Me neither," Cherish added.

"I am feeling a little tired."

The three girls looked at Florence.

"Please come back soon, though?"

"We will," said Joy as she collected her sisters' teacups.

After they had gone, Florence breathed a sigh of relief. Sometimes she really missed them, but now she realized how nice it was to be away from them. Her life was as close to perfect as it could be.

ON THE WAY back to the house, the girls decided to save the news that Florence was having a baby until their mother came back from visiting their sisters.

CHAPTER TWENTY-NINE

*B*y the time Spring rolled around, Florence's drainage work had begun on her property with her father's good friend overseeing the work. Together they'd made a plan of the orchard and it was finally starting to come together, at least on paper.

Florence could no longer hide her baby bump under her regular clothes. It would've been much easier in her old Amish dresses.

She hadn't seen her sisters for a couple months and when she saw Cherish running toward her, she knew that she had news of either Honor or Mercy's baby.

Florence hurried to meet her.

"It's Mercy, she's had a boy," gasped Cherish between breaths.

"Oh, that's wonderful news! What did they call him?"

"That's not all. Honor's in labor and she'll have hers anytime. She already knows she's having a boy, too."

Florence was overcome with emotion and tears streamed down her face. She'd changed Honor's and Mercy's diapers and now they were mothers. It seemed like only yesterday that they all lived under the one roof. She wiped her eyes. "Pregnancy hormones," she said to Cherish.

Cherish giggled. "*Mamm* is really happy. I don't know when she'll be back. Maybe never."

"She'll be back. Don't worry."

"I'm not worried, but I'll have to wait until she comes back before I go to the farm again. I daren't ask Levi for anything. Anyway, enough about me. How is the morning sickness?"

"Gone completely."

"That is good and you're getting bigger." She rubbed Florence's tummy.

Florence laughed. "I know. Um... what did *Mamm* say about me and Carter having a baby?"

"We haven't told her yet. We're waiting until she

comes home."

"Ah, that's probably best."

"She can concentrate on them and when she gets home, we'll tell her."

"And, how's the orchard?"

"I don't know. When I'm not at work, I stay away from the house pretending I'm looking for work. I mostly do look for work, so I won't be lying."

"Good."

"Florence, can you come here a minute?" a man's voice called out.

Florence turned around. "Coming."

"Who's that?" Cherish whispered.

"Eric Brosley. He was an old friend of *Dat's*. He's giving me a ton of help in setting up the orchard."

"I'll let you go then. It's good you get to use bull-dozers and things. We'd never be allowed."

Florence looked over at the equipment. "It's some kind of digger, but it's not a bulldozer."

"Yeah, well all the same to me. Forbidden."

Florence stepped forward and hugged Cherish. "Thanks for telling me about the babies."

"I'll come back and tell you when Honor's has arrived, and the names they've chosen."

"Okay, thanks."

THREE WEEKS after the babies were born, Wilma returned.

She arrived, in tears saying she was already missing the babies.

Joy, Honor, and Cherish had all cooked a special dinner in honor of *Mamm's* homecoming and Ada and Samuel, and Mark and Christina came.

They made their mother's favorite chocolate cherry cake for dessert along with a choice of apple pie. For the main meal they had baked pork roast with crackling skin, and side dishes of apple sauce, sweet potatoes, and spinach. Cherish had made a hot chicken, mushroom and pasta dish called tetrazzini.

Even with all the effort they made and Levi being nice, their mother hardly smiled.

"We're pleased to have you home, Wilma. Our nightly readings haven't been the same without you," Levi said.

Wilma nodded. "I'm glad to be back."

"*Jah,* you've missed so many of them. We have one every night except on Sundays." Cherish said, resisting the urge to roll her eyes. No one was happy about the enforced readings since they'd all rather read alone. Even Joy preferred to read on her own. At least she and Isaac were able to do that now in their caravan.

"*Ach, Dat,* are we having a reading tonight? We have guests."

Levi smiled. "You're right, Bliss. We'll give the nightly reading a miss tonight."

Ada nodded. "*Gut* idea, Levi. Now, tell us more about those *bopplis,* Wilma."

Wilma's face lit up. "They're so small and they look exactly alike. They'll grow up like brothers, or maybe even twins. I miss them so much." Wilma's eyes glistened and Ada passed her a handkerchief and she wiped her eyes.

The girls were aching to tell their mother about Florence and Carter having a baby but couldn't do it until their guests left. They'd already asked Christina and Mark to keep quiet about it.

"Did you miss us while you were gone, *Mamm?*" Cherish asked.

Mamm looked up at her. "Well, let me think ... *Nee.*"

Everyone laughed, even Levi.

It was Cherish's hope that when her mother found out she was going to be a grandmother for a third time, she'd open her heart to Florence and Carter.

That night, the girls didn't get a chance to have a private word with their mother. Ada and Samuel stayed until late, and as soon as they left, *Mamm* and Levi went to their room.

The ideal time came in the morning, just before Hope left for work. Levi was still in bed and Joy had stopped in for coffee after Isaac had gone for work. The four Baker girls were there along with Bliss.

"Mamm, we have something to tell you."

"What's that?" She looked across the table at Hope, who'd been appointed the spokesperson.

"It's about Florence."

"Florence?"

"What does she have to do with us?" Bliss asked.

"Florence and Carter are having a baby."

Mamm gasped and covered her mouth. *"Truly?"*

"That's right."

"I'm happy for them."

"And we're happy for you, *Mamm.* You're a three times *grossmammi,"* Cherish said.

"I have to go to work, or I'll be late. Excuse me." Hope ran out of the house.

Their mother adjusted her *kapp,* pulling it forward on her head. "The only way you could've found out is if one of you is talking to her. Do you think that's wise?"

"She's our *schweschder.*"

"Half," *Mamm* corrected. "And your *vadder* wouldn't be happy with what she's done with her life."

"That's right, *Mamm,*" said Bliss.

Cherish was disappointed, wondering if their father would be happy for Florence and Carter, and looked across at Joy who looked equally sad. Favor just sat there scowling at Bliss for butting in, and for calling their mother "*Mamm.*"

HOPE PEDALED down the driveway hoping her mother would finally talk to Florence. If everyone talked to one another, it would be a better life for all of them. Fairfax was there parked on the side of the road in the same place he'd waited for her these past months. He jumped out of the driver's door when she approached, ready to place her bike in the bed of his truck.

After months of Fairfax taking her to and from work in secret, Hope was starting to see that Fairfax might possibly join them one day. There was a chance. He'd said he was making positive changes in his life and his quest had led him to think more about God. On their short drives to and from work, he'd asked her many questions about the Amish lifestyle and beliefs about God.

She sat in the passenger seat and a minute later, he sat beside her. "My mother got back last night, and we had a big dinner. Everyone came. Well, not everyone."

"Yeah, I wasn't there."

It had been a sore point between them that their relationship was a secret. "Well, they don't know you. I mean they know *of* you. You bought the horse from Levi and you met the family."

He shrugged and moved his pickup onto the road. "I guess that's a start."

"It is." She knew something more was bothering him. "What's the matter?"

He swerved the vehicle to the side of the road and stopped. He killed the engine and then looked at her. "Where's this going? I know you like me, but you won't be seen anywhere with me. Won't even have a cup of coffee or a meal with me. I just want you to be my regular girlfriend. Can't we have a normal relationship?"

She gulped. She didn't want to lose him. "I told you at the start we couldn't be seen together."

He pushed his head back into the headrest. "This

is madness." His hazel eyes flickered with disappointment. "I want us to do things together. Go for a walk in the mountains, hold hands. Go canoeing, go swimming. Do things that regular folks do when they're dating."

She bit the inside of her lip. "I'll be late for work. Can we talk this afternoon?"

"Don't you feel anything for me?"

"Yes. You know I do, but things are a bit rocky in my family at the moment, and if they find out about you, they'd throw me out of the house. I'm sure of it. We're living under Levi's laws and my mother doesn't even have a say."

"Then move in with me."

She gasped. "I couldn't."

"You could. Stop letting them run your life. Think for yourself. You're old enough."

"I do think for myself."

He rubbed her arm. "I'm sorry. I shouldn't have said that. I know you do. I'm just frustrated about this whole thing. I want us to progress and move forward. Are we going to be doing this for years— snatching minutes together, hiding away like we are?"

"It's hard, I know."

"I want to invite you to dinner at my folks' place."

"I can't."

He started up the engine. "I know."

The rest of the drive to work was silent. Hope wasn't even sure if he'd come for her in the afternoon. When she got out of the truck, she leaned down and said to him, "You could always join the community."

"I couldn't live like that. I'm sorry, Hope."

Immediately, she regretted asking him that outright. "Bye. Will I see you this afternoon?"

"Yeah, sure."

She closed the door of the pickup and walked into the building without looking back.

Business was brisk at the Bed and Breakfast now that the warmer weather had arrived. That meant Hope was kept non-stop busy and for that she was thankful. There wasn't too much time to worry about whether she'd see Fairfax again.

While she ate her sandwich during her break, she wondered what life would be like if she left the community. Florence had done it and it'd worked out for her, but she'd been older and had known Carter for a lot longer than she'd known Fairfax.

At two o'clock, going-home time, she walked out

of the building and spotted the pickup truck in the parking lot. She walked over to him, having made up her mind that she couldn't leave him hanging on. It was too hard for both of them.

When she opened the door and slid into the passenger seat, she was surprised he was smiling. "This is a change."

"I've decided to give it a go."

"What?"

"Joining the community."

"Wait! What?" She wasn't sure she'd heard right. People didn't just join like that. As much as she'd dreamed about it, prayed about it, she didn't think it would happen. "It's more involved than you think."

"I'm over the modern world."

She couldn't contain the giggle that escaped her lips.

"I'll talk to your bishop before I go further."

"Yeah, that might be a good idea. Don't mention me. He'll get the wrong idea if he thinks you're joining for a girl."

He drew his eyebrows together. "I can't start off on the wrong foot. If he asks me, I'll have to tell him." He started the engine and moved onto the road.

She couldn't help smiling. Was this really happening?

FLORENCE COULDN'T KEEP her eyes open any longer so she lay down on the couch. She soon drifted to sleep. She didn't know long she'd been asleep when she was awakened by soft knocking on her door. In a still-groggy half-asleep state, she opened it to see Wilma.

Florence saw her stepmother standing there looking radiant and lovely in a pale blue dress with a fresh white starched apron and cape. On her head she wore a pretty prayer *kapp,* and Florence guessed that Christina must've made it for her. The strings of her *kapp* flapped in the breeze. Before Florence could speak, Carter came to stand behind her.

Wilma smiled at Florence and then turned her gaze to Carter. "Could you forgive a silly old woman? It was easier to turn my back than to face that I gave you to my sister to raise."

Florence had doubts about what Wilma said, remembering that she'd encouraged Christina to give her child away. When she turned and saw the look of delight on Carter's face, she knew she had to keep those thoughts to herself.

Wilma continued. "I'll never be your mother because Iris has that place in your heart."

"I know," he said, smiling brightly like Florence had never seen him smile.

"I don't want to replace her, but I might make a … a friend, an aunt, or a babysitter if you ever need one."

Florence wiped a tear from her eye. Wilma had heard about the baby. That news must've tugged at her heart. Florence had once thought it easier to get the orchard back than for Wilma's heart to soften this far.

Suddenly, the orchard seemed far less important.

Family was what mattered.

Carter turned and looked at her. Then he reached out and touched her shoulder. She frowned as he started shaking her. "Florence, are you okay? Florence, wake up."

Florence opened her eyes to see Carter crouched down next to her. She realized she was lying on the couch and she bolted to a seated position.

He put his hand on hers. "You were talking in your sleep and seemed upset."

"Wilma … is she here?"

He frowned, looking puzzled. "No ..."

She looked around. It was just the two of them and she was on the couch. Her hands went to her forehead and she rubbed her temples. "I must've been having a dream. Wilma came here to make amends. She wanted ..." she looked into Carter's eyes. "She said she'd blocked you out."

"I didn't want to wake you, but there's nothing worse than a bad dream." He moved to sit next to her and enclosed her in his strong arms. She rested her head on his shoulder. "Forget about Wilma, Florence. It doesn't matter what she thinks, or what she does. Iris was my mother. You're all the family I'll ever need. We have each other, and we have our baby. We also have Spot, when he's awake."

She giggled. "I know," she whispered.

Family *was* what mattered. Her family was right there with Carter and their baby, who was growing inside her.

I hope you enjoyed Their Amish Stepfather.

If you'd like to be updated with new releases and hear of special offers, add your email at my website: https://samanthapriceauthor.com/

Blessings,
Samantha Price

Find out what happens next for
Florence and the Baker Girls in:
Book 9 (The Amish Bonnet Sisters).
A Baby For Florence

ABOUT SAMANTHA PRICE

A prolific author of Amish fiction, Samantha Price wrote stories from a young age, but it wasn't until later in life that she took up writing full time. Formally an artist, she exchanged her paintbrush for the computer and, many best-selling book series later, has never looked back.

Samantha is happiest on her computer lost in the world of her characters, and is best known for the Ettie Smith Amish Mysteries series and the Expectant Amish Widows series.

www.SamanthaPriceAuthor.com

Samantha loves to hear from her readers. Connect with her at:

samantha@samanthapriceauthor.com

www.facebook.com/SamanthaPriceAuthor

Follow Samantha Price on BookBub

Twitter @ AmishRomance

Instagram - SamanthaPriceAuthor